Because of the explosion, all of the amusement parks closed early, driving out the entire community of panicked tourists. News vans and first responders also created congestion, sharing the same destination. Rush hour on its worst day didn't compare to this chaotic ride.

Upon driving closer, Minka and Renee could see the smoke ascending from the twenty-three-story building. Totally engulfed in flames, the Orange County Courthouse lacked its former majestic quality. Firefighters surrounded the south side, where the thickest smoke bellowed into the sky. The darkness of it, combined with the late hour, filtered the whole scene, but the detectives managed to find Cael and his partner, Declan Schuster. Having arrived minutes ahead of Minka and Renee, Gus stood with the guys.

Minka swallowed the lump in her throat. "I can't believe this is happening here."

Praise for Karina Bartow

BROTHER OF INTEREST:
"The author did a good job of revealing one clue after another, much like peeling back the layers of an onion…If you like a good mystery with deep personal relationships, you will enjoy this book."

~Author Jan Sikes

~*~

"Author Karina Bartow shows the many aspects of often complicated family relationships in detail—and does it brilliantly."

~Kat Henry Doran, Wild Women Reviews

~*~

"It had just the right amount of mystery, suspense, and likable characters."

~Author Ruth Roberts

~*~

WRONG LINE, RIGHT CONNECTION
"The story is fresh and entertaining, and I enjoyed it from start to finish."

~Reviewer Sammi Cox

Accidental Allies

by

Karina Bartow

Unde(a)feated Detective Series,
Book 3

Accidental Allies

Cover Art by *Tina Lynn Stout*

The Wild Rose Press, Inc.
PO Box 708
Adams Basin, NY 14410-0708
Visit us at www.thewildrosepress.com

Publishing History
First Edition, 2023
Trade Paperback ISBN 978-1-5092-5207-7
Digital ISBN 978-1-5092-5208-4

Unde(a)feated Detective Series, Book 3
Published in the United States of America

Dedication

To all my allies out there:
thank you for believing in me.

Prologue

Minka and Wes Avery drove their five-year-old daughter, Caela, to her first day of school. The little girl babbled during the whole ride, excited to start kindergarten. Minka shared her exhilaration, but sorrow overpowered her glee. She couldn't help but reflect on how fast the time had gone.

Without realizing it, she began to tinker with the transmitter for her cochlear implant in her ear, a nervous habit she developed as a kid. Her daughter didn't waste time pointing it out to her. "Mom, why are you turning off your cochlear on me? You only do that to Daddy and Uncle Robin."

Wes wagged his finger in front of Minka's nose.

"I would never do that to you, sweetie," she responded. "You have way more insightful things to say than they do. I just had an itch."

Caela accepted the explanation and continued to prattle on. Meanwhile, Minka returned to her reverie, thinking back to the day after she resigned from the police force and how she busied herself with setting up the nursery. She didn't admit it to anybody, but she sat down on her glider at one point and mused, "This is it?"

Of course, that sentiment dissipated real fast after the baby arrived. Now, she struggled with the brevity of those quiet moments, and she asked the same question but with a whole new meaning.

When they arrived at the charter school in Orlando, she and Wes escorted Caela to her classroom, where they helped her locate her cubby and desk. Her teacher, Mrs. Wetzel, greeted them, but since they met at the open house the night before, she darted off after a few words to tend to other children. Once Caela settled into her chair and began to chat with a girl beside her, Wes nudged his wife toward the door. She considered pretending she didn't register his hint, but being a former detective, she couldn't get away with playing dumb.

In an effort not to become a blubbering mess as they exited, she ran through the to-do list she set up to distract her from her sadness. She used to hope to have a new baby to fill the void, but her negative pregnancy test last week showed there wouldn't be a little one anytime soon. For the first time since her days as a rookie policewoman, she struggled to map out her present life course.

Trotting out of the school building, they headed to their SUV. Right before she hopped inside, she spotted her former commanding officer, Gus Channing, and his wife, Lola, in the next aisle of the parking lot. She directed her husband's attention to them, and they strolled over.

"Hey, you guys. Did you get Ryan squared away in first grade?" she asked of their son.

"With some major negotiations." Gus shook his head. "I think I've had easier interrogations with criminals than I do coercing the boy to behave for the teacher."

Lola folded her arms. "He took a disliking to her from the instant they met. What can I say? He's his father's son."

Gus gave her a teasing jab in the side. "Remember who's the law enforcer here."

She giggled before addressing Minka. "How'd Caela do? Any tears?"

"Only mine." Minka swiped away the evidence under her eye. "She's ready for anything, but five years wasn't enough to prepare me."

Lola embraced her. "I cried all the way home last year, too. Would you like to go get coffee?"

Minka nodded. "As long as you can give me a lift home."

Her friend agreed, and Minka wished Wes a good day at the School for the Deaf where he taught biology. Before they all parted, Gus took a step toward Minka. "Detective Stratford just told me he's retiring at the end of December, so I reckon we'll be taking applicants in the next few months. Just thought I'd give you a heads-up, in case you're searching for a way to keep occupied while Caela's in school."

A smile crossed Minka's lips, and her glance at Wes revealed he wore one, too. "I'll think about it, Lieutenant."

Chapter One

Four Months Later

As Minka set the table for her dinner party, her mind spun through everything she needed to do in preparation for her big return to the Orlando Police Department the next day. In truth, the last thing she needed was company as it added to her load, but she owed it to Gus. When at least three other officers deserved a promotion, he'd taken a big risk by referring her for the job.

Caela's footsteps shuffled across the hardwood floor. "Can I help, Mommy?"

"Yes, you can. Why don't you put the napkins in their rings, and after that, we can frost the cake for dessert."

The little girl beamed, revealing that the second task delighted her most. She rushed to secure each napkin into its holder before she zipped into the kitchen. As always, most of Caela's contribution ended up in her mouth, and her lips were covered in chocolate by the time she finished.

When Wes entered the room to lend a hand, he retrieved a disposable napkin from off the stack. "Let me clean you up, sweetie."

As Caela approached him, he acted like he was going to dab it off. At the last second, he buried his head into her face and layered her with kisses, making her break into a fit of giggles.

Minka stepped around them, careful to keep a firm grip on the serving tray. "Daddy beat me to it."

She checked on her biscuits to determine if they were golden enough yet, and satisfied with them, she twisted the knob on the stove. She put on her oven mitts to remove the pan but had to strip them off right away when her cell phone rang. As she predicted, the screen read her brother's name. In order to keep working, she switched on the speakerphone. "Hey, Robin. Are you on your way?"

"No, I'm sorry. I can't make it. I'm on a case."

She figured as much. Now a bounty hunter, he always had someone on his radar. "Which one?"

"Did you hear about the dude who stormed onto the launch pad right before the last blast-off at Cape Canaveral? Somebody gave us a tip that he's back in town for the birth of his kid, so my competitors are posted at every hospital in the county. Meanwhile, I'm betting he and his wife will opt for a home birth and am staking out their condo. He has forty grand on his head, so if I catch sight of him, I'm busting in there. I don't care if I trip over the kid's umbilical cord or slip on the—"

Minka's gaze slid over to Caela. "Your niece is listening."

To her relief, he caught on to the message and withdrew his usual graphic narrative. After swapping greetings with Wes and Caela, he told his sister, "After tonight, you'll be sniffing out leads, too. You just won't get the payday I do. I'm glad I compared the salaries before I made it too far along in the academy. That place evoked some bad memories of grade school, man. Anyhow, sorry I won't be there, but I read the article in today's paper."

Her eyes widened. "You read the paper?"

He snickered. "A couple of my buddies sent me the link."

"I'm popular in the bounty hunter community? And my daughter claims I'm not cool." She stuck out her tongue at Caela.

"Well, we like cops who bring people to justice. We just appreciate it when you flub up the apprehending part."

"Says the man whom I caught hiding in my garage when he was evading the authorities," Minka reminded him.

"But you didn't discover me for nearly a week."

She shook her head but didn't address the matter. "I appreciated the article, but it adds to the pressure."

Her stomach churned from nerves as she recalled the write-up in the paper her brother referred to. Titled *OPD Welcomes Back Renowned Deaf Detective*, it summarized her entire career, up until she *traded in her gun for a baby bottle.*

"What pressure?" Robin questioned. "I thought you loved being a cop."

"I do, but it's a little scary. I mean, I haven't worn a badge in over six years."

Caela joined the conversation. "What are you talking about, Mommy? You've had your old patrol one in your purse."

Minka raised her brow. She only used her souvenir from the police department—which nobody was aware she kept—under extenuating circumstances. "How do you know that?"

She grinned, her brown eyes glimmering with mischief. "Well, you used it to get out of a speeding ticket that one time. I also saw you show it to the kid who was being mean to me on the playground."

"You were three years old on both those occasions," Minka cried.

Wes clapped his hands with pride. "I told you, she inherited your skills of perception."

Minka smiled and gave her daughter a high-five. "Just don't tell those stories to Uncle Cael or Gus."

"I won't. I never tell you the things I have on them."

"And she inherited your skills in hustling," Minka said to Wes.

Her husband beamed, and she directed her attention back to Robin. "Well, I wish you the best tonight. If you strike out, you might want to try the launch pad. Once he realizes the tough job fatherhood is, he may try to escape the planet again."

Robin chuckled. "Thanks for the tip, sis. Congratulations, by the way. I'm proud of you. Life has offered you a lot of chances to sit back and take things easy, but you never have. You shouldn't worry at all about proving yourself. You've done that already."

While touched by his sentimental side, she still couldn't resist her urge to tease him. "As long as I don't have to hunt my own brother down again, I suppose I'll manage all right."

"I guess I'll give you a few weeks to get broken in before I rob that bank I've staked out."

She laughed and thanked him before hanging up. Within a few minutes, the doorbell rang, and Wes rose to let the Channings in. As seven-year-old Ryan dashed around his parents, Caela caught up to him in no time. Like always, the two rushed upstairs to play in her room. Minka smiled as she observed them, glad they maintained their bond despite their many differences.

Minka and Wes greeted Gus and Lola, and the couples settled into the living room. They fell back into their typical patter, exchanging stories about work and the kids, along with Minka's reunion with the police force.

Lola patted her friend on the knee. "So, are you ready for your big day tomorrow?"

Minka drew in a deep breath. "I suppose so. After all these years of playing an armchair detective, I'm hoping I haven't lost my knack for being a real one."

"I have no doubts, which reminds me—" Gus fished out her old detective's badge from his pocket. "—I had enough faith we'd be here someday that I saved this for you."

She accepted it. "Faith or stinginess?"

He grinned. "Both. For what it's worth, I even shined it up for you. It beats that old, scratched one in your purse."

"How do you know what's in my purse, Lieutenant?"

"Your daughter told my son."

Minka crossed her arms. "According to what she told me just before you arrived, she has dirt on you, too. Guess I'll have to weasel some out of her."

They shared a laugh, before Lola asked Minka, "Are Cael and Autumn coming?"

"Not anymore. Tyson's running a fever, and even though they think his teething is behind it, they decided to stay home just in case. They're pretty exhausted, anyway," she reported of her brother-in-law's family.

Lola glanced toward Gus with a smirk. "A baby calls for a lot of adjustments."

Her comment and the glimmer in her eyes intrigued Minka, making her scrutinize Lola. The sweater poncho Lola wore didn't fit with her usual style, but the chilly January breeze merited an extra layer. Even so, she didn't don many frocks that were as baggy as this one. Plus, she'd declined the wine Minka presented before they sat down.

Minka couldn't tell whether or not her commanding officer perceived her suspicion, but he changed the topic. "Renee gave me a call on our way and said they'd be late. They'll eat dinner on the road and join us for dessert. She said she would've let you know, but she doesn't have your number."

"I invited her, so she should," Minka replied.

Her tone must've given away a hint of irritation, as he seized the chance to give her some authoritative input. "Listen, I realize this is going to be a much different partnership than yours and Cael's, but I suspect you two will get along well. And if you don't, keep in mind she'll be retiring in a couple of years, so just try to stick it out."

Minka took a sip of chardonnay. "Sounds like the talk I gave Caela about her art teacher on her first day of kindergarten."

"What can I say? Like mother, like daughter."

She acknowledged his point and stood to put the finishing touches on dinner. With nobody else to wait on for now, they hollered for Caela and Ryan to venture downstairs. Once everyone dug into the meal, Lola circled back to Minka's return to work.

"I know you said Wes gets done teaching his last class an hour before Caela's released from school, but if something ever delays you, Wes, I have no problem picking her up. My offer still stands to take her in the morning, too, if you'd like."

"Thanks so much, but her heart's pretty set on riding the bus in the morning," Minka said.

"Like I've wanted to since the first day of school," Caela piped up. "But Mom never let me."

Minka mussed her daughter's light brown locks. "Isn't a mother's love the worst?"

The adults chuckled, before everyone fell silent for a moment and chowed down. Gus made a light mention of some of the precautions they implemented at the station in the wake of recent threats from protestors around the city. A series of wrongful arrests and mishandled police responses in other departments led to complaints of racial profiling as well as calls for better training regarding mental health crises. For the most part, Orlando's Chief of Police and other officials remained silent on whether or not they'd meet the outcries for policy changes. The demonstrators, of course, interpreted that to signal a lack of action.

Minka and Wes had discussed the new risks associated with working in law enforcement multiple times before she accepted Gus's offer. Together, they concluded the dangers, though different, always existed, even back when Minka applied to the academy. She took on the duty with her eyes wide open, and the experience she had behind her better equipped her to handle them now.

Like Gus, Minka chose her words with care

because of the children nearby. "Besides the extra security guards, has the city council agreed to upgrade the surveillance system?"

"Not officially, but I reckon we're getting close."

"I hope you inform them we're running out of places that sell VHS tapes," she joked of the outdated equipment. Then, somberness struck her. "Has all of this affected your approach to the job? Does it fulfill you as much as it used to?"

He nodded. "Being under a microscope does take a toll if you concentrate on it, but the key is not to let it consume you. No matter what you do in life, somebody will always be around a corner, criticizing you, and you can't let that determine the joy you reap from it."

The comment lured his son into the conversation. "And I keep telling you pranking people brings me joy, Dad. Why should I stop?"

"Because if you don't, your mother and I will suffer heart-attacks from all the calls from your principal. Then, you'll be out the joy—and food and toys—we add to your life." Gus cocked a smile at Ryan, who didn't offer a rebuttal. He redirected his focus to Minka. "Sure, we've both witnessed cops misuse their power, but we aren't them. We have the opportunity to show people that it's not a blanket category. Haven't you had some experience in proving people's perceptions wrong?"

She leveled a sly grin at him, appreciating the advice. She dropped the subject, but Caela surprised her mom by continuing the shop talk. "Was your very first day as a cop exciting, Mom?"

"Not really. I was excited, but nobody else seemed to want me there. No one believed I could do my job because of my deafness."

"Not even you, Uncle Gus?"

"I hadn't met him yet," Minka explained. "I was working in Atlanta, but I didn't find anyone like Uncle Cael or Gus. They couldn't accept what made me different, which is why Daddy and I tell you to give everyone a chance, no matter how they look."

The girl nodded. "Did they fire you?"

"No, they didn't." Minka refrained from detailing how the department wanted to keep up the appearance of instituting an equal-opportunity employment policy.

"How'd you get here, then?"

She debated how much she should reveal. "There was a girl, Claire, who lived in the apartment next to mine. We didn't see each other very much, but when we did, she would say nice things to me about me pursuing my dream. She mentioned her cousin, who was a detective in Orlando."

"Uncle Cael," Caela stated.

"No, it was me," Gus replied. "That was before my promotion to lieutenant."

"Anyway, Claire dropped her phone outside her door, and I kept it for her to return it the next day. She didn't come home, though, so I answered it when Gus called because I was worried about her, and we found her together. Then, he asked me to move here and work for him."

Caela gave Gus a thumbs-up. "Good decision."

He winked. "One of the best I ever made."

While they reverted to chitchat, Minka's mind trailed off to that day she first spoke to Gus—as well as the parts she couldn't share with her innocent child...

For two days running, Minka knocked on the door

to Claire Pennbrook's apartment with her neighbor's phone in her hand. Since Minka had found it, the device kept ringing with calls and messages. Minka didn't examine any of them out of courtesy for the woman's privacy but wondered if Claire was calling her own phone as a means of determining its whereabouts.

She didn't detect any more activity than she had since she retrieved the phone. And the note she'd written yesterday, asking the young woman to stop by or call, remained in the same spot where she taped it to the door. Even so, she waited for several minutes, hoping it would eventually swing open. Consulting her watch, she realized she couldn't dally for much longer without causing a scene as her other neighbors departed for work. With her luck, some busybody was bound to call the police and report her. That would land her a warning from her captain about taking on such a matter with her "circumstances," as he liked to say.

She shuffled away from the apartment, but before she made it too far, Claire's phone rang. The screen displayed Gus Channing's name, which Minka recalled was Claire's detective cousin. She still hated to impose on her neighbor's private life, but her growing concern compelled her to answer it. "Detective Channing?" she greeted him with uncertainty.

He hesitated, no doubt taken aback by a different voice. "Yes. Who is this?"

"Minka Parker, Claire's neighbor. I work with the police department, and I found her phone by her apartment door a few days ago. I've been holding onto it, but I haven't caught her at home since."

"I'm glad you answered, Officer Parker. My family's been worried sick about her. The last time she and her mother—my aunt—talked, Claire expressed fear that somebody was following her. Given what you just said, I'm afraid she might've been right."

Now, as she peered over at Gus, Minka bubbled with gratitude for his willingness to give her a chance, both back then and now.

"Cake time!" Caela announced, jolting Minka out of her reverie.

Aware of her daughter's eagerness to play more, she agreed to serve the kids now, with the adults waiting for Renee Hart and her husband to arrive. The boy and girl both scarfed down their dessert with the efficiency of sharks. As anticipated, they asked their parents to be excused, and they all obliged the plea in an effort to let them work off the sugar buzz before bedtime.

They continued to await the Harts, neither of whom Minka met before. The older woman transferred from the Miami department two years earlier, so Minka had no idea what to expect of her new partner. She worried she could have the same mindset as the officers in Atlanta, who stereotyped her and deemed her unfit for duty. Like Wes kept pointing out, however, she encountered those unknowns when she was partnered with Cael, and that enriched her life more than she could've fathomed.

At last, a knock echoed against the door, and Minka trotted over to answer it. She smoothed out her blouse, tucked a stray strand of her auburn locks back into place, and expelled a cleansing sigh. When she opened the door, the older couple wore smiles, but she could sense their apprehension. Upon locking eyes with Renee, she observed the uncertainty in them, but she figured hers didn't beam with confidence, either. The woman appeared to be in her mid-fifties, her salt and pepper hair clipped back in a barrette. She gave a timid smile and extended her hand.

"Come on in," Minka greeted. When Wes took her side, she began the formal introductions. "I'm Minka, and this is my husband, Wes. Wes, meet Renee and..."

"Cliff," Renee replied.

The guys shook hands, and Minka mused over the contrasts between the husband and wife. Trim in build, Renee stood refined in her black suit, whereas husky Cliff slouched a little in his well-worn overalls. Above his grisly beard, his eyes seemed kind, and Minka could already deduce he was the laid-back one in the marriage.

Minka led the pair to the dinner table, where Gus and Lola welcomed them. They exchanged small talk, but despite Gus and Renee's working in the same precinct, they didn't seem very well acquainted. In a way, it helped the meeting, as they learned about one another together. Cliff and Renee shared that they married thirty-seven years ago and raised two sons and a daughter. When the kids descended the stairs for a drink, the Harts offered kind smiles and a few words, before Caela and Ryan scrambled back to their games.

As they enjoyed the cake, Renee cleared her throat and shifted toward Minka. "I've heard a lot about you. You made quite an impression in your short time as a detective."

Her emphasis on *short time* made Minka wonder whether or not she should take it as a compliment. "I appreciate that."

"After all, not many people get away with taking a

six-year-long maternity break, especially in our line of work."

The statement made it clear she didn't have a great opinion of her younger partner, but Minka handled it with professionalism. "I realize that. I'm very thankful to Lieutenant Channing for even considering me for the job. When I resigned, I didn't know if I'd ever be back on the force, but I really wanted to stay home with my daughter."

Renee pursed her lips. "Some make that choice. For my part, I never missed a day of work on my children's account. It taught them responsibility."

Among other things. An awkward silence ensued over the group, until Lola volunteered to clear the empty plates. Minka assisted her, and after they loaded and started the noisy dishwasher, she used the opportunity to vent.

"Can you believe that woman? Here, I worried my deafness would give her the wrong impression of me, when she ends up judging me for my choice to stay home and raise my little girl."

Lola snorted. "Welcome to Motherhood Central. We keep the population going through labor pains and sleepless nights, only to get disgruntled kiddos and criticism from strangers."

Minka giggled. "You must not think it's that bad, considering you're giving it another go."

Lola's mouth dropped, and her hand instantly fell to her middle. "Did the poncho give it away?"

"That and you refraining from your favorite wine."

Lola smiled. "And you're afraid you've lost your touch as a detective."

The ladies hugged, and Minka congratulated the

mother-to-be, who bound her to secrecy for the time being. The door's sudden movement threatened their new pact. As Gus stepped through, his serious expression interrupted the celebratory mood.

"There's been an explosion at the courthouse. Minka, you're officially on duty."

****

As eager as she'd been for her first case, Minka couldn't suppress her nerves. Her job rarely, if ever, dealt with minor matters, but she didn't expect to resume her career on such a dramatic note. This would be a national headline, ironically just like the case of the missing basketball players, the last major investigation she headed up before she relinquished her badge.

Driving her partner across town, Minka's anxiety level rose more due to Renee's cold demeanor. To give her the benefit of the doubt, Minka supposed it could just be her way of showing her commitment to her job, especially since it was such a serious one. Plus, the insane traffic compounded the nightmare scenario and didn't lend to an atmosphere of kinship. Because of the explosion, all of the amusement parks closed early, driving out the entire community of panicked tourists. News vans and first responders added to the congestion, all sharing the same destination. Rush hour on its worst day didn't compare to this chaotic ride.

Upon driving closer, Minka and Renee saw smoke ascending from the twenty-three-story building. Totally engulfed in flames, the Orange County Courthouse lacked its former majestic quality. Firefighters surrounded the south side where the thickest smoke bellowed into the sky. The darkness of it, combined with the late hour, filtered the whole scene, but the detectives managed to find Cael and his partner, Declan Schuster. Having arrived minutes ahead of Minka and Renee, Gus stood with the guys.

Minka swallowed the lump in her throat. "I can't believe this is happening here."

"Nobody's off-limits," Gus stated.

"Have we learned anything yet?" Renee asked.

"Just that everyone nearby heard the explosion around seven o'clock, and whatever caused it was clearly on the south side. Could've been in one of the offices over there or, more plausibly, the parking lot back there," Cael told them.

"Was anyone inside?" Minka questioned.

Gus shook his head. "Thankfully, with it happening on a Sunday evening, the building was empty, except for the night guards on duty. One of them was taken to the hospital, but the others are fine."

Minka took a step back, wanting to minimize the smoke she inhaled. "Have they identified the cause?"

"Not yet," Declan replied. "For now, they're focused on containing it. I, for one, highly doubt that a staffer left their hot plate running."

Renee spread out her arms in confusion. "But if it was intentional, why do anything when everybody's gone?"

"As a message, and we aren't counting on this being a lone incident," Gus said. "The bomb squad's on their way, just in case there are any more surprises in the area. We've already called the FBI and Homeland Security."

Minka reflected on the threats going through the city, but she didn't want to believe protests would escalate to an act of terrorism. The idea of her hometown being under attack made her wish she could be home with her family, like she did as a young girl on September eleventh. Only in her early teens, she didn't have a husband and daughter to worry about, though. Back then, she simply wanted the protection of her parents' arms and assurances that everything would be fine. Now, she shifted into the role to protect her family, along with thousands of others.

In an attempt not to let the weight of the situation overwhelm her, Minka asked, "Did the guards spot anyone suspicious?"

"We spoke to all three who are here, but none detected anything unusual," Cael answered.

"Didn't somebody patrol that lot?" Renee asked.

"He showed up late to work," Declan told them.

The statement raised Minka's distrust. "Did you guys talk to him?"

Declan nodded. "Yes, and he claims to have an alibi. We haven't made contact yet, but we have nothing else on him."

"What about surveillance?" Renee questioned.

"Maybe some of the areas where the cameras are still intact will give us something. I doubt we'll be able to recover any footage near the blast, though," Cael said.

Having appeared at the courthouse a number of times, Minka visualized the surrounding businesses. "We should ask for the diner's footage across the street."

Her fellow officers agreed with a mere nod, but until the dust settled, they couldn't do anything except peer at the efforts to salvage their city's symbol of justice. All the while, Minka could only wonder if it would be repaid with the same justice it'd strived to mete out to others and what the city would encounter in the meantime.

****

The light from the television flashing under the bedroom door sent guilt through Minka for keeping her husband up so late. The alarm for both of them would be going off in just over three hours, and the sleep deprivation didn't seem very worthwhile at the time. The bomb squad uncovered the remnants of a pickup truck that they suspected harbored the explosives, but the detectives couldn't find anyone who spotted its entry. After that, they headed to the precinct in case a lead surfaced. They didn't meet with any success, however, and neither did Gus in his attempts to collaborate with the feds.

Upon opening the door, Minka couldn't help but stand and admire the scene, a most touching one after witnessing destruction all evening. Caela lay nestled against her father, both sleeping in peace. As news coverage about the explosion continued to play on the television, she snuck the remote from Wes's firm grip and hit the power button. Ironically, the lack of noise roused him from his slumber.

"I'm sorry," she whispered, crouching down beside him. She smiled at their tranquil little girl. "I'm glad to see you weren't lonely."

"Yeah, the bombing really scared her. I tried not to let her see what happened, but it was impossible. Any leads?"

"No, other than the fact that we suspect the bomb detonated in a truck. Nobody witnessed anything, though. We haven't had any direct threats about the courthouse, and neither has the FBI or Homeland. I suppose the protests should've warned us. I just can't bring myself to admit we've been attacked. This is our home."

He drew her close and kissed her head. After the moment passed, she threw on her pajamas and climbed into bed by her daughter's side. Caela didn't fully awaken, but Minka could sense her contentment when she rolled over and cuddled into her.

Nevertheless, Minka struggled to fall asleep, unable to rid the devastating images from her mind. She realized it could've been so much worse, especially in a city with such major attractions, but the experience still carried a heavy blow. She'd always understood that true security was only an illusion, but she managed to convince herself she had more control over her own than the average citizen. This, however, exposed her vulnerability.

When morning arrived, Minka had to set her emotions aside and deal with the situation as a law enforcer. In a convenient coincidence, Caela's school had a teacher in-service day, so Minka dropped her off with Wes's mom, Jacqueline. Given the dire conditions surrounding the town, she didn't experience the nostalgia she anticipated upon parking in the station's lot. Once she entered the building in the light of day, she realized how much had changed during her hiatus. While the pale blue walls and oak wood furniture remained, she didn't recognize most of their occupants. Gus and Cael kept her informed of the departures and transfers of her former colleagues, but she didn't process the overall turnover until she stood there.

Few people seemed to notice her, but she didn't take offense. The precinct buzzed with activity and nervous energy. Though the FBI was conducting their own investigation of the bombing, Orlando PD still had the duty to protect its citizens and apprehend any threats to them. With Cael and Declan working with CSU to determine if any evidence could be recovered from the truck in question, Minka and Renee trekked to the diner across from the explosion site.

When they parked beside the eatery, a lone truck occupied the lot, and they observed the poor owner evaluating the damage to his property. Fallen debris covered the ground and tables in front of the restaurant, and some shrapnel broke a window. His grimace and drooped posture revealed he didn't welcome guests at the moment. "I'm sorry, but we're closed," he said sharply without raising his head.

"Not to police, you're not." Renee displayed her badge as the man pivoted toward them.

His face lost its agitation when he noticed Minka. "Minka?"

"Dawson," she greeted her old friend from the police academy, walking up to hug him. "Looks like you've switched career paths."

"Yeah, the force really wasn't for me after my wife had our third child," Dawson Michaels explained.

"You have three kids already?"

He smiled. "No, seven; we just had quadruplets last summer."

"Goodness! I can barely keep up with one," Minka exclaimed, laughing, but her jovial moment was cut short by her partner's judgmental scowl. "This is Renee Hart, my new partner. Renee, Dawson Michaels. We graduated from the academy together."

If Dawson perceived the tension between the women, he made a smooth transition back to the investigation. "It's just crazy. I resigned from the department to be safer for my family, and there's an explosion right across the road from my diner."

"Nobody was here at the time, I take it," Minka said, aware they only served breakfast and lunch.

"No, but it was close. I had a late delivery come in, so I'd only left about half an hour before everything happened. It was all over the news by the time I made it home."

"And you didn't notice anything out of the ordinary in the area?" Renee questioned.

"Not that I recall. I mean, I was focused on getting home and wasn't looking around too intently. Once you're in a routine, everything just blends together."

Veering back to their initial motive for the visit, Minka asked him, "Do you think your surveillance cameras might've captured the parking lot over there?"

"Our front lot here is monitored, but the camera doesn't capture farther than the road."

Since the perpetrator would've driven the truck with the bomb to the scene at some point, they asked for the footage in hopes of catching sight of it enroute. After wrapping up with Dawson, the detectives spoke to the manager of the hotel next door and the guests who stayed overnight. Nobody offered additional insight into the incident, and they all had solid alibis. Nonetheless, they asked for the building's surveillance footage, as well.

Before they returned to the courthouse, Minka scanned the area again and spotted an older mansion on the other side of the diner. Over the years several businesses had occupied it, but it now stood empty. A large For Sale sign hung in front of the building.

Minka gestured toward it. "Do you suppose that place would have any surveillance?"

Renee crossed her arms. "Nah. In fact, I see a mount that probably used to hold a camera on the porch's ceiling. It's not worth the hassle of tracking down the realtor. Besides, the hotel and diner provide just as good of a vantage point as that would."

Minka accepted the logic and strode with Renee to the ravaged courthouse, where the security staff constituted the only sign of life. Despite the smell of smoke still permeating the air, they conducted a few interviews but treaded lightly since the employees remained in shock. Once they concluded, they proceeded to request a copy of the surveillance from the previous day.

Back at the precinct, they began viewing the footage. As expected, the cameras near the explosion site were completely destroyed, along with the evidence they may have provided. An unharmed one on the southwest corner of the building was angled just enough to catch a glimpse of the vehicles entering and exiting the lot, though it was a fleeting one. Even so, that appeared to be all they needed when Cael and Declan called with a development.

Cael reported CSU's findings on the make and model of the truck they suspected carried the bomb before he shared further details. "Looks like it recently had a botched paint job. They were able to recover a small piece of it on the wheel well. It's burgundy now, but the original color was lighter."

"The common criminal never likes to overpay for service," Minka replied.

Thus, they commenced the hunt for the pickup in question. Minka slowed down the footage in an effort to capture a better view of every vehicle. Before long, they spotted a trace of it arriving fifteen minutes before the bomb was detonated. From both that angle and the diner's, the license plate was obscured, but something else grabbed Minka's attention.

"Did you see that?" she asked Renee, backing up the incriminating video. "They didn't just barge through the gate, like we predicted. They stopped and swiped an access card."

"Do you think it's an employee?"

"Either that, or somebody posing as one."

Grabbing her phone, Minka called the courthouse security department. While the blast destroyed the card reader, she hoped they'd offer insight into who drove the truck if it belonged to an employee. The man she spoke to gave her that and more.

"One of my guys, Tyler Gill, drives that," the supervisor stated. "He's the one who showed up late to work last night—coincidentally, claiming he had car trouble."

Chapter Two

On the road within minutes, Minka had to do a double check to ensure she had the right address. Upon their approach, a lone garage, surrounded by beat-up cars and trucks, awaited them. The tags on the plates of the two vehicles in the driveway revealed that they hadn't been driven—at least legally—in years.

After noting the second story above the garage, Renee suggested it could be an apartment. They walked up to the side door and pounded on it as hard as they could, for fear nobody would hear them if they were upstairs. Just when they began to conclude it wouldn't pay off, Gill answered, reeking of alcohol.

"How can I help you lovely ladies?" he slurred.

"Detectives Hart and Avery, Orlando PD," Renee greeted with sternness. "We're investigating the explosion at the courthouse last night, and we couldn't help but notice your tardiness in arriving at work."

He snickered and mocked her terminology. "You going to put it on my grade card, teacher?"

"I might put it on your criminal record, if you're the one who placed a bomb in your pickup and set it off once you planted it in the parking lot."

"The same lot you were supposed to be patrolling," Minka added.

"Wait, what about my truck?"

With growing impatience, Renee said, "We found a

bomb inside it."

Gill remained calm, shrugging. "Oh, well, I didn't put it there. I don't even have the piece of garbage anymore. I took it to the junkyard last week, where it belongs."

"That's convenient," Renee replied, gesturing to the collected vehicles in the lot. "You scrap the one that's used to explode your workplace but hang onto all these other rust buckets."

"They're classics, lady!"

Unimpressed by her partner's methods, Minka took a more diplomatic approach. "Which junkyard did you take it to?"

"The dump on Colonial."

Minka notated the claim. "Your boss mentioned that you had car trouble last night, which is why you arrived late. Can you explain that?"

"I wanted to drive my beauty over there, but something was wrong with the ignition switch. I tinkered around with it for a while before I had to give up and take my station wagon."

"Can anybody verify that?"

"My best bud, Kirk O'Connor, right there in that brown house across the road. He strolled over to lend me a hand."

They took their leave and headed to O'Connor's bungalow, but all the while, kept an eye on Gill's place, afraid he used this as a ploy to give him time to escape. He didn't need to, with his neighbor holding up his alibi. Still before noon, their big lead had died quicker than it'd been born.

While driving back to the precinct, Minka tried to make conversation. "I'm not sure a lush like Gill could even devise a plan like this."

"I am," Hart said. "A drunk has a bad day at work, starts researching how to make a bomb, and the rest is history. I'm sure we could've dragged a confession out of him, had he not been reminded of his alibi."

She may not have accused her partner, but Renee's tone made it clear she disapproved of Minka's methods. Back straightening, Minka reminded her, "His neighbor corroborated it."

"Didn't you smell the booze on that guy? He was as plastered as Gill."

Minka's staying power wore thin. "Guess I blew the case, then."

Renee recoiled a bit, a Cheshire cat grin crossing her lips. "I wouldn't go that far. I just wouldn't get so chummy with persons of interest if I were you."

You could've fooled me. Keeping that thought to herself, Minka decided her partner referred to their conversation with Dawson—who wasn't a person of interest, she wanted to point out. Not eager to get into a sparring match on their first day working together, she kept her mouth in check and apologized.

After they arrived at the station, they broke for lunch, which they enjoyed separately. Cael and Declan hadn't returned from their assignments, so Minka couldn't have joined them even if she wanted to. Stewing over Renee's biting remarks, she decided to call her husband, who was also on his break. She related her drama with Renee, despite predicting he wouldn't display his support in the way she wished.

He lived up to her expectations. "Well, I can understand her cautioning you to keep an objective view of somebody so close to the crime scene. After all, you haven't seen Dawson in years. I don't have to remind you of the classmate of mine who lured me into the grips of her mobster boyfriend."

Minka rolled her eyes at the memory of all that led to Wes's brief stint in witness protection. "Dawson is no Shantelle Braydon. He's too busy with all those kids to be in the mob."

"True. Caela alone keeps life chaotic enough. By the end of the day, I'm too bushed to stay awake for the late-night talk shows, much less meet a crew down by the docks to take care of business," he said, impersonating the voice of an old Italian man.

She couldn't help but giggle. Her spirits brightened, until she glanced at Renee across the room. The waves of despondency rippled back in. "I just don't know if Renee and I will ever be compatible."

"So, you didn't get off to the best start. That's typical. Not everyone's my perfect little brother."

She sighed. "Her remarks about my extended maternity break last night just unnerved me."

"She's probably a bit jealous, honey. My guess is, she has a terrible relationship with her kids, and maybe, deep inside, she wishes she would've walked away like you did. Plus, she might even envy you for your skills. I mean, she's twice your age and hasn't been promoted in probably decades. I'll bet that's the reason for her snarky comment about you only being a detective for a short time. You just need to get into a rhythm. I'm sure you and Cael did, too."

"Yes, all of about thirty seconds," she agreed, before being interrupted by another call. "Speak of the devil. He's on the other line. He might have a lead. Love you."

"I love you, too."

She clicked over. "What's up?"

"CSU says the bomb in the truck never detonated," Cael told her. "Something else caused the explosion."

****

As disconcerting as the situation already was, the latest development put a damper on the investigation. Without insight into where or what kind of explosives were used, the task of finding the culprit became even more daunting. Only two hours earlier, they had the cause of the explosion along with the suspect's vehicle. Now, both seemed worthless.

So as to leave no stones unturned, Minka and Renee poured over all of their footage again, including the video from the diner. Although the bomb in the truck hadn't detonated, its presence was suspicious, possibly being a back-up plan, if needed. The detectives cued up the diner's video recording to the time when the pickup arrived at the courthouse. Viewing the rear end this time, they spotted that its license plate had been spray-painted to conceal its numbers.

Keeping in mind Gill's claim about scrapping it, they placed a call to the junkyard to confirm his statement and learn if they sold it to anyone. The owner found it in their records then, after he consulted with one of his employees, he informed them the truck had already gone through the crusher. Hence, the truck carrying the bomb had to belong to somebody else.

"Unless he's lying," Renee stated.

"We have no reason to doubt him."

"Of course we do. He's a necktie away from being a used car salesman."

Ignoring her stereotyping, Minka reasoned on the

facts aloud. "Whoever drove that truck no doubt knew Gill had one just like it. Maybe they even painted it to appear to be his."

"That's a lot of trouble to go to for a bomb that never went off."

"I'm still not sure that was the plan. Either way, was Gill supposed to be just as much of a victim in this as the courthouse?"

"It wouldn't be hard to imagine someone take a disliking to him," Renee agreed.

Minka suppressed a grin over the irony of Renee's allusion to her own dislike of him. Despite their uncertainty over what kind of condition the drunk would be in by now, they headed back to Gill's house. They found him working on the car he said he couldn't start the day before. A beer can sat at his feet, but he seemed to be in better shape than earlier.

He peered in their direction as they trotted across the overgrown lawn. "You two are back? Did my folks put you up to this gag?"

Renee bit right on his poor choice of words. "Do you consider terrorism a gag, Mr. Gill?"

His foolish smile faded, and he took a step backward. "No, ma'am."

Minka wished she could stay mute and thereby avoid Renee's indignation if she phrased something wrong, but she mustered her courage. "The junkyard where you took your truck confirmed that it's gone through the crusher, but we still spotted one that looked just like it entering the courthouse last night. We think someone painted it, maybe to frame you. Do you have any inkling of who might have it out for you or possibly carries an issue with someone inside the courthouse?"

He shrugged. "My ex-girlfriend's a little cuckoo, but I didn't even own the truck or work there when we dated."

"Who else has seen you in the truck?" Minka asked.

"Only a handful of people, as a matter of fact. I didn't drive it anywhere but work or when I needed to haul something."

"Have you been on bad terms with a coworker at all, past or present?" Renee questioned.

He shook his head, before his glazed eyes lit up with discovery. "I did have an odd incident happen about a month back. Man, why didn't I think of that weirdo sooner?"

Minka could only guess what kind of character this guy would deem a weirdo. "Someone at work?"

"No. One night, I was browsing through classifieds online for a side-job. This listing popped out at me, practically made for me. It asked for insider information about the courthouse, with an incentive of ten grand. I offered my expertise right away, but the guy acted so strange. He layered me with questions about the building's layout, then wanted a copy of the blueprints. That smelled fishy, so I told him no way. I could get fired for that."

"Did you get the person's name?" Minka asked.

"No, I just used his account name. I think I still have an email." He extracted his phone from his cargo shorts and accessed the message. "Yeah, this is it: Collector25."

"Could you forward me your back-and-forth with him?" Minka asked and spelled out her address.

He asked her to stop and repeat herself a couple of

times, blaming her speech impediment, but his inebriated state couldn't have helped. Afterward, she gave him a command she hoped he'd remember once he sobered up...whenever that may be. "If something like this ever happens again, be sure to report it to the authorities."

He saluted her, eliciting a groan from Renee. As they drove back to the station, Minka read through the emails between Gill and Collector25. While Gill told the truth about refusing to cooperate in the end, he didn't have the pure motives he let on to them. Sure, he raised the objection of endangering his job, but he used the threat as leverage to get a better offer. He haggled for at least twenty grand, but the buyer wouldn't budge on his original price.

Minka opted to keep mum about his willingness, considering he complied with their request. When they arrived at the precinct, they called the classifieds website in an attempt to learn who lay behind Collector25. To their disappointment, the account was now closed and irretrievable, even to the site's managers. With that source exhausted, they decided to explore the pseudonym Collector25 on different online marketplaces. No accounts were listed under the name, so they ran it through a general search engine, which didn't yield any results of value.

Minka studied the moniker, hoping for a breakthrough. "Twenty-five. Could be their age, how long they've been married, or..."

"Or their address," Renee suggested, standing beside her.

"That'd be pretty foolish, don't you think?"

"I've seen worse. Now, we just have to figure out

if it's a house number or street. Could even be highway twenty-five."

"That narrows it down," Minka muttered. "I'm starting to think this is an older person. I mean, he had to involve an insider to get the blueprints, instead of hacking into the courthouse. I can't picture a younger person doing that."

"Are you saying all young people are hackers?"

Minka ignored her partner's demeaning tone. "No, but even if he didn't have the skill set, someone young would be more prone to hire a professional."

"Let's leave the profiling to the feds."

Minka repressed the childish urge to stick out her tongue at her partner's rigid ways. During the rest of their shift, no further leads materialized, making the afternoon crawl. When the day ended, Renee murmured a muffled goodbye, and they parted their separate ways. As Minka dabbed away a helpless tear, Cael texted her to invite her, Wes, and Caela over for dinner.

Relieved not to have to cook, she took a quick shower when she arrived home, using hot water to relax her weary body. She dressed and was reapplying her makeup when Caela joined her to chat about her visit with her nana. To Minka's surprise, she never mentioned the explosion, her blissful innocence a refreshing change after the grueling day.

She did her best to maintain a carefree spirit when she and her family entered Cael and Autumn's house. While she didn't usually consider her sister-in-law's presence as a way to unwind from a stressful day, she expressed her appreciation for Autumn's last-minute hospitality.

"I'm glad to do it. I figured you'd need a night off

after all the craziness. What a way to resume your career." She rolled tofu tacos, which Minka could only hope she could coerce her daughter—and husband—to try. "From the little I've heard from Cael, it sounds like this is only the beginning."

She feared Autumn's words would prove true, but she didn't want to discuss work. Holding her ten-month-old nephew, she changed the subject to him. "At least Tyson feels better today. I see another tooth broke through."

"Two did, actually. Between that and his colic, he's been louder than those man-eating Rottweilers next door."

Minka chuckled at the cat lover's remark. "I remember it well."

"That reminds me—" Autumn retrieved a bowl from the fridge and offered it to her sister-in-law. "—I read the other day that sweet potato skins increase fertility, so since I fixed some last night for dinner, I figured I'd save ours for you."

Once again, Minka regretted ever confiding her pregnancy dreams in her. Since she'd mentioned trying to conceive right after Autumn found out she was expecting Tyson, Autumn considered herself a guru on the matter and loved imparting her wisdom to Minka. Thus, she regulated—or attempted to regulate—her diet, exercise, and even brewed up a concoction of herbs that rarely stayed down. Hungry, exhausted, and nauseous, Minka suffered all of the symptoms of pregnancy with none of the perks.

Needless to say, the sight of soggy, half-eaten leftovers didn't appeal to her stomach. "Thanks, but I can make my own. To be honest, we really aren't trying right now, with my going back to work and all."

"Yes, I know, but it never hurts to keep it on your mind. When you do, your body sees how important it is to you and may eventually cooperate."

Minka nodded, like she always did when Autumn waxed philosophy. Still, she couldn't stifle a chuckle the instant Autumn vacated the room.

Cael entered and scrutinized Minka's expression. "I suppose I should be happy you're smiling, but it scares me when you do it around my wife."

"I'm finally beginning to understand why you married her: she makes you look sane!"

Noting the dish on the counter, he sighed. "I begged her not to keep those."

"It's okay. She gave me the first laugh I've had today."

"I doubt many of us found much humor in anything today. I'm sorry we didn't give you a nice homecoming. What do you think of Renee?"

Minka shrugged. "I get the feeling she doesn't like me. She made this snarky comment last night about me staying home with Caela for so long."

Cael gave an intuitive nod. "That's probably because her daughter was killed last year by a drunk driver. The poor lady hasn't been the same ever since. Worse yet, the driver was some politician's son, so everyone handled him with gloves. He only had to serve community service and five years' probation. The whole deal tore Renee apart."

"I can imagine," she acknowledged, appreciating the insight into her partner's rough exterior. "Maybe things will get better after this chaos. Did you make any breakthroughs with the guard in the hospital?"

"No, he's still drifting in and out of consciousness. From the little he could say, he barely remembers the blast. He did manage to tell us Gill showed up late on a regular basis. The other guards confirmed that."

At first, she dismissed the statement but then stumbled on a connection. "We already suspect that the perp knew the truck he drove and mocked one up to look like it. What if they also witnessed his unpunctual habits?"

Cael caught her drift. "That would give them an idea of when to make their move."

"And it'd all take some scouting out. The diner would be the optimal place to do it, too. Renee and I might head over there tomorrow and ask for some more surveillance from the past few weeks."

"Are you sure you don't just want to see Dawson again?" he teased.

****

Tuesday morning, Minka's new status as a working mom set in, with Caela having to get ready for school. She tried to prepare everything after they returned home from Cael and Autumn's, and she retreated to bed satisfied, convinced she covered it all. The light of dawn exposed what she missed, however. Beyond comprehension, she overlooked her top to-do of packing Caela's lunch, a simple chore that carried the threat of major implications. For months, she and her picky daughter battled over food choices, and she'd just begun to master the art of compromise.

Wes, who typically played neutral Sweden in the negotiations, offered his assistance, and Minka agreed. A maniacal grin crossed her lips, eager for her husband to get a taste of the ordeal. Her devious delight didn't last long, with the echoes of the ruckus that ensued traveling up through the ceiling. While she tried to fashion her hair in peace, she plucked out her cochlear transmitter to spare her nerves. The instant she did so, her conscience needled her over her promise to Caela about never taking it out because of her, so she reinserted it.

Her makeup applied, Minka put on her watch and shoes to finish her outfit. She headed downstairs and sighed when Caela's protests told her the whole lunch conundrum marched on. She figured she'd have to be the one who ended it. She descended the stairs and made her way toward the kitchen, hoping not to be hit by flying food when she entered.

"I'm not a mind reader, sweetie," Wes reminded his daughter.

"I can see that, Dad!"

"What's the problem here?" Minka asked.

"I'm handling it," he told his wife.

Caela crossed her arms. "No, he isn't."

"You're the one who needs to start learning what things are called, instead of just, 'What Mommy bought beside the milk at the store,' " he argued.

Minka translated the request with ease. "The fruit parfait."

"Finally!" Caela cheered, glaring at her father.

Throwing it in with her grilled cheese sandwich— cut vertically down the middle, with no crust, as she always insisted—he handed the lunch box to her, and she skipped into the living room. Wes leaned back on the counter in exhaustion, as Minka chuckled and gave him an appreciative hug. "You can feel free to take her grocery shopping, too, so you'll understand what she's talking about," she said, the errand not among the mother-daughter moments she cherished.

He kissed her. "No, thank you, Detective."

She whipped up a sandwich for her own lunch, before Caela announced her uncle's arrival. Minka and Cael used to ride to work together every day but given he didn't mention resuming the habit even last night, she didn't anticipate him dropping by.

"Hey, Booger Face," Cael greeted his niece, using the nickname he gave her when she had a cold as a toddler.

Caela replied by stomping on his foot, a custom she started performing not long after he adopted the hated moniker.

Minka ignored the rituals between them, used to their antics. "What are you doing here?"

"I wanted to see this little monster get onto the bus for the first time, and I figured you and I could drive in together, for old times' sake. If I'd anticipated a welcoming like this, though, I might as well have stayed home with my colicky baby and grumpy, sleep-deprived wife."

Wes gave him a hug. "I'm happy to see you, bro."

"So am I, but I just figured Declan would be riding with you," she explained.

"He doesn't mind driving on his own this once."

Minka agreed to his offer, happier than she portrayed. She embraced the chance to start the day with a sort of normalcy, given all the surrounding madness. Before they strolled off to the bus stop, she, Caela, and Cael said goodbye as Wes departed for work

She kept up a strong front, but the sight of her little girl boarding the bus and waving from her seat tugged at her heart even more than she predicted it would. From her vantage point, mere seconds had passed since she nervously strapped her newborn baby into her car seat for the first time. She worried it'd only feel like a few blinks more before she'd be helping her grown daughter into a limo enroute to her wedding.

After the bus drove away, Minka and Cael made their way back to the house. She dabbed a few tears off her cheek, and he put his arm around her shoulder, prompting her to lean on him. Of course, Camille Paleta, the busybody of the neighborhood, emerged from her house right as they strode by. Her watering can in hand, she did her best to douse the tender moment. "My! I could only wish to get along with my in-laws so well."

"I bet the feeling's mutual," Cael replied.

She stammered a bit, but apparently, her craving for fresh insight into their lives helped her ignore the insult. "I read the article about your return to the police department, Minka. Congratulations."

"Thank you, Mrs. Paleta," Minka replied, having to remind herself not to slip up and call her Scoop, as they often called her due to her thirst for the first scoop of gossip about her neighbors' business.

"So, has being a housewife run its course, or are you and Wes having financial struggles?"

"We're trying to save enough money to buy a house next to a nice quiet monastery," Minka nearly told her. Instead, she said, "Neither. The opportunity just arose, and we decided to take it since Caela's in school now."

The woman furrowed her brow. "And you don't have any desire to grow your family?"

Cael played interference, pointing his thumb at Camille. "Man, Minks, I think we could take a few tips from her on interrogation techniques."

Camille sneered but used the disparaging remark as a springboard into more gossip. "I bet you're flooded with interviews after the other night. My husband and I were about to go to bed when the bombing happened, but my daughter called to alert us. What a horrible thing. I'm grateful it didn't kill anyone, but why would somebody do such a thing at night?"

"We believe it was to send a message without inflicting too many casualties," Minka told her.

She nodded. "My hairdresser assumed the same. She said that'd be an effective way to minimize the risk of staging such an attack."

"I trust you put your interrogation skills to good use and asked for her alibi," Cael said.

Minka smiled while Camille again floundered, but they didn't give her the chance to recover this time. Advancing back toward the house, they wished her a nice day. Minka managed to bottle her laughter, but she let it burst out once they retreated inside.

"Nobody could've convinced me you'd be the one to dish out her comeuppance instead of me," she remarked in between cackles.

He shrugged. "After you endure weeks of your infant screaming louder than a chainsaw all night, a blabbermouth old lady doesn't intimidate you very much."

Minka retrieved her lunch, tablet, and purse before they headed to the precinct. Once they arrived, they split up to join their respective partners, with Minka longing for the days when they shared the same desk.

She repressed her nostalgia and tried to keep an open mind about Renee as she approached her. After she greeted her, she discussed her plan to make another trip to the diner in order to determine if anybody was spying on Gill. While she didn't commend—or even verbally agree with—her logic, Renee didn't challenge her idea. Her lack of enthusiasm disappointed Minka, but she did her best to trudge through it, remembering Renee's grievous state.

They didn't spend long at the diner, given Dawson had repairmen there to address some of the damage. Even so, he obliged them and handed over a month's worth of security footage. Since the diner was always closed by the time Gill reported to work, they wouldn't have much trouble spotting suspects. On the very first day they viewed, a white sedan appeared during the right time frame, but it proved only to be the cleaning lady. They observed her intently, not wanting to take her innocence for granted, but she didn't give the courthouse the slightest glance.

Two weeks into the recordings, they noticed a young man who accompanied the maid, seeming to be commissioned to assist her. He helped her unload her supplies, but soon, his lackluster work ethic became evident. Once the woman carried in her vacuum, the teenager leaned against the car, texting away.

Renee let out a tsking sound. "Typical kid."

Minka agreed with her for a change, until the boy started peering at the courthouse and took a picture of it with his phone. Then, he walked across the street, vanishing from the camera's view for just under ten minutes. The woman exited the diner to reprove him for his sluggishness and lured him back to his assignment.

"What do you think he was doing over there?" Minka asked her partner.

"Could've been talking to someone, or just goofing off, or…"

"Or plotting. We have to find out who this kid is."

Finishing their review of the last two weeks of footage, they discovered he returned with the woman twice more, only to have him manifest the same behavior. Minka called Dawson to learn the lackluster assistant's name. He reported the maid was his aunt and the boy, her stepson.

"His name's Kiefer Limburg. He's a weird dude. Doesn't get along with anyone in the family, but he has quite a following online. We all joke that it's because none of them have met him in person."

"So, he's big into social media?" Minka asked.

"Yeah, he has like 300,000 subscribers. I've watched a few of his videos, but they're not for me."

"What are they about?"

"Mainly conspiracy theories," he informed her, making her brow rise. "He's always been cynical, but once he took government and civics in school, he really spiraled. In fact, he didn't even graduate because they expelled him his senior year for starting a protest and planting a cherry bomb in the superintendent's office."

Every word pointed to Limburg as capable and eager to commit a crime like this. Minka asked for his information, including links to his online profiles. While she related the details of their conversation to Renee, she located his page and began to scan through his vlogs. They browsed his feed and soon spotted one with the courthouse as its backdrop. It bore the title *Orlando Florida—Really the Dreamiest Place on*

Earth? Posted one of the days his stepmom took him to work, his words were chilling, considering he spoke to them less than a week before the bombing.

"Orlando—The City Beautiful in the Sunshine State: Yeah, Orlandoans have a one in fifteen chance of becoming a victim of a crime, giving us a crime rating of two. Sound good? Maybe so, until you realize that's on a scale of one to one hundred, with one hundred being the safest. That means we're safer than two percent of the cities in the country. Yay, us.

"Why would such a family-friendly place be so dangerous? Behold the building behind me. Ladies and gentlemen, I give you the Orange County Courthouse, making criminals' dreams come true. Every year, drug dealers, murderers, and just the common dirt bags walk in a felon and leave a free man. Meanwhile, innocent victims never get justice because of the inept judicial system in this county.

"Yes, this massive building serves as just an ornament in a city where the beauty and magic tourists babble on about are lies. In reality, it's every man for himself, because this glorious center of justice fails to protect even children. We might as well burn it to the ground and rebuild one right inside an amusement park, so it can finally be the fairy tale it truly is!"

"Sounds like he's about to unveil the summer's newest attraction," Renee stated.

"Yeah, I think we ought to ask him for a sneak peek," Minka declared.

Chapter Three

Wasting no time, Gus sent out a call to detain Limburg and get him to the precinct immediately. The officers in the neighborhood of his address responded and carted him in, cuffed, within thirty minutes. While he didn't resist arrest, he entered the building with insults and choice words flying, charging the department with many of the same accusations he ranted about online. Needless to say, Minka and Renee didn't hurry to join him in the interrogation room.

Minka sucked in her displeasure as she sat down across from him. "How's this for the setting of your next vlog, Mr. Limburg?"

He peered around the room, wearing a rebellious sneer. "It's perfect. I've always wanted to broadcast from the epicenter of justice at its worst."

"What an honor," Renee replied. "I thought you gave that title to the courthouse."

"Well, they can only work with the little they're given from you morons."

Ignoring his gruesome lack of respect, Minka continued, "So, you show your indignation of the way criminals are treated by becoming one? You want to be Exhibit A in terrorists eluding the law?"

"Last I checked," he said, "speaking the truth isn't an act of terrorism."

"Bombing a government building is," Renee said.

The kid lost his rebellious sneer. "What are you saying? You think I was behind the courthouse explosion?"

"You clearly had it out for the institution," Renee replied. "And with your stepmother working across the street, you'd have enough access to formulate your plan."

"I wasn't even there that night, and in fact, I don't think she was, either. I don't really mean the things I say online. I just want more views."

Minka crossed her arms. "You make empty threats to the government for all of the world to see, simply to be popular? Then, you're shocked that somebody considers you a suspect when one's executed?"

"I didn't do it!"

His insistence only made Renee strike harder, as she slid a photo of the injured night guard's grandson across the table. "You rant and rave about innocent children being robbed of justice, and here, you set off a bomb that nearly crippled this little boy's grandfather."

"I wouldn't do that. My grandpa died on 9/11." His voice cracked. "He was a first responder and was trying to get people out of the north tower when it collapsed. That's why you have to believe me that I'd never do a thing like this."

His tears moved Minka. "We're sorry for your loss."

Her partner slid over a glare. "You still shouldn't be making threats online, though."

"My vlogs are just an outlet. I know it might sound un-American of me, but I've always blamed the government for what happened to my granddad and so many other parents and grandparents that day. I'll never be able to even meet him, so this is how I cope. Call me whatever else you want, but I'm no terrorist."

"If you weren't at the courthouse the night of the blast, where were you?" Minka asked.

Limburg hesitated, before he admitted, "I was tagging some buildings with my friends."

****

Minka and Renee stepped into Gus's office and related their conversation with Limburg in an attempt to decide how to proceed. By the time they finished, the lieutenant spelled out their only option. "If his alibi checks out, we have to let him go."

"Can't we at least charge him for decimation or something?" Renee replied.

"Sure, but that doesn't bring us any closer to solving this case."

Minka sighed. "There goes another big lead crumbling into a pile of nothingness."

Renee dropped her head, but when she raised it, her eyes brimmed with fiery determination. "I still say we should arrest Gill. He's the prime one with means and opportunity. He just suckered his friend into holding up his alibi and paid off the junkyard to say they'd crushed his truck."

"The bomb in it wasn't even detonated, though," Minka reminded her.

"It was his back-up plan. I say we tell the press we landed our bomber and get them off our backs."

"Man, you have quite the sense of duty!" Minka cried.

Before she could make a counterblow, Gus played interference by asking Renee to go and release Limburg from custody. Since he didn't excuse Minka, she stayed in place, assuming he'd take the opportunity to give her a lecture.

When he simply sat and gazed back down at his book, however, she questioned him, "Where's the finger-wagging?"

"What finger-wagging?"

"I just insulted my partner. That warrants a disapproving *Minka* if nothing else."

"Fine: Minka, respect your partner. Good enough for you?"

She sat down at his desk. "Suddenly, I'm the voice of reason in my partnership and now even with my tough, no-nonsense boss. I don't like this dream."

"I guess I'm not myself today. Drop by tomorrow, and I'll reprimand you then."

"I'd rather you reassign me then," she said, still testing him. When he once more gave no reaction, she stood, but before exiting, she snatched the book he was studying and examined the title. "Prepping for the captains' exam, are we? Good for you."

Gus shrugged, seizing his manual. "Yeah, well, I don't have much of a choice."

"What do you mean?"

"The chief called earlier, and he has several other candidates more qualified than me to take over the precinct."

"Why?"

"We've butted heads on more than a few issues lately, and a terrorist attack hasn't helped matters. He's unsatisfied with where we're at in the investigation. Says we should have a solid suspect by now."

"We've had two in two days, for Pete's sake. It isn't our fault they both have shady but solid alibis.

Besides, why don't the feds bear any weight in this? They haven't produced anyone of interest."

Gus shrugged. "I think he feels under the gun to give the city results. Since we're not giving him any to pass on, shaking things up like this is the best way to appease the public."

"Until the criminals start taking advantage of a mismanaged police department," Minka stated. "I'm calling him and giving him a piece of my mind. None of this is your fault."

"Minka, please, don't. I have to handle this myself. The other guys he's threatening to elect as my replacement are all captains, so I figure I'll take his trump if I pass the exam. It's my best shot."

She understood his feelings but couldn't form a suitable response. With a sinking heart, she stood again to leave, but before she opened the door, she expressed, "You were the only reason why I stayed on the force as a rookie and one of my biggest ones for giving it another go now. I never could've made it this far without you, and I don't know what this job would mean to me if you weren't here."

He leaned back in his chair. "Thanks, Minks."

She nodded and strode out to her desk, all the while reflecting on Gus's first act of faith in her…

Like she'd promised Detective Channing during their initial conversation, Minka confronted Captain Detwiler about Claire Pennbrook's disappearance. She explained what the detective told her about Claire's family being unable to get ahold of her and their fears for her safety. No matter how much she told him, however, her commanding officer refused to give credence to her narrative. Since nobody made an official report on Claire, they mustn't get involved in a petty family dispute, according to him. He advised Minka to just drop off the phone at her building's lost-and-found desk.

Minka remembered trekking out of his office with her shoulders slouched. She couldn't help but assume he didn't take stock in the matter because of her handicap. She tried to replay the sentiment her parents drilled into her, that he was the one with the disability if he couldn't overcome his stigma. Deep down, though, she believed she was the failure, as she failed Claire and Detective Channing. Deflated by Detwiler's briskness, she struggled with the task of calling Gus back. Nonetheless, she remained resolved to keep her word to him.

"Hi, Officer Parker."

His continued use of her title planted a grin on her lips, as no one referred to her like that, besides her parents and a few friends. "Hello, Detective Channing. I'm sorry to tell you I haven't made any progress here."

She summarized Detwiler's response, fighting to maintain a respectful tone. He made understanding replies, which added to her guilt over disappointing such a kind guy.

"I appreciate your help, Officer. I'll just keep doing what I can on my end. I'll call your precinct and file a report. I should've done that days ago, but I just kept hoping my aunt overreacted. I'm sorry I put you in this position," he said.

"Please don't apologize. I can empathize with your family's desperation. My brother went missing for a couple days when we were kids." Saying the words made her remember why she became a cop in the first place—to help people like Robin. Whether she was assigned to it or not, she had that precise opportunity at her fingertips. "Could I do anything to assist as her neighbor?"

He paused. "My aunt's been worried over a recent breakup Claire had with her boyfriend, Justin Harris. I guess he's dating a pretty possessive girl now, and my aunt wonders if she could be involved. Did you ever meet him along your run-ins with her?"

"No. Claire mentioned being on her way to a date once, but I never observed them together."

"Would you mind digging into him and contacting him if you can?"

She gave a defiant glance toward Detwiler's office. "Sure."

In light of the way Gus rescued her from an unfulfilling career, Minka determined to do whatever she could to vindicate him from unjustified scrutiny.

****

Even after she returned home from work, Minka remained tense. With her mind on Gus's promotion predicament, her anxiety drained her of the desire to cook or help Caela with her homework. Wes's failure to assist with either task miffed her. Once they put Caela to bed, she sat down to skim through her notes on the case again.

Wes seemed to recognize her frustration at last and joined her on the couch. He rubbed the space between her shoulder blades. "What happened with your person of interest, that kid you were about to interview after lunch?"

"Turns out, he was doing something illegal, but it had nothing to do with the bombing. He's just a good ol' street artist."

"Sorry, babe. I'm confident you guys will nail whoever's responsible before long."

Minka almost let the moment pass, unsure Gus would want Wes to be aware of his troubles, but she couldn't keep it inside any longer. "I'm afraid it may not be soon enough. The chief of police is in the hot seat over all of this and is about to use Gus as a scapegoat. He already has a list of possible replacements."

"That's ridiculous. This isn't his fault. If anyone should be fired at this point, it should be the head of security at the courthouse."

She nodded in agreement. "Now I feel more pressure than ever to solve this. Of course, it's my first case in six years, and I wouldn't even be surprised if the chief brought that up, too. Gus's decision to rehire me wasn't popular with many."

"Don't get ahead of yourself."

She grabbed ahold of his hand when he offered it. "It's just hard. He gave me my start and then, a second chance I didn't figure I'd get. I can't let him lose what he's worked so hard for on my watch. I owe him that."

They sat in silence until Minka's phone rang. She recognized the name and clicked on it immediately. "What's going on, Gus?"

"For one, CSU has determined a trio of pressure cooker bombs was the real cause of the explosion."

"Do they have any clue where they may have detonated?"

"Yeah, after some examination of the worst affected area, they unearthed the remnants in Judge Nichols's office. Bet you can't guess who his brother-in-law is."

His remark intrigued her. "Who?"

"Tyler Gill."

"No!"

"Guess we can do the math on how he landed the job," he stated.

"So, what does this mean? Could he have been setting Gill up?"

"He would've known what Gill drove, so he fit that part of the criteria. On the other hand, I highly doubt Nichols would be dumb enough to carry a bomb to work and then put it under his desk."

"He could've taken it in after hours," she suggested.

"True. Regardless, I want you and Renee to meet with Nichols and see what you can gather from him."

Minka wondered what Renee would make of the development. Because of the way her partner kept trying to pin the bombing on Gill, she expected this to aid her campaign against him. Her desperation to close the case—with or without all the facts—troubled Minka. She worried, after so many years on the job, Renee lost her passion for the truth and cared more about making an arrest than righting a wrong.

She dismissed the notion, striving not to attach bad motives to her partner. She already struggled enough to get along with her. She called Renee with the update, but Renee didn't manifest the delight Minka predicted. Instead, she seemed perturbed by both the disruption to her evening and the fact that Gus relayed the news to Minka rather than her.

By morning, she appeared to be over it, and they rode together to the judge's house. With the courthouse still closed, all hearings were postponed, and the staff worked remotely. Renee knocked on the door of his century-old Victorian, and he answered it with a smile, as if it were any ordinary day off. The judge wore his bathrobe and sweatpants, giving no visible indication of the tragic week. "Hello, Detective Hart. Detective Avery, it's good to see you back on the force. Our city needs your dedication."

His cheery demeanor puzzled her, given the week's events, but Minka tried to mask it. "Thank you, Judge."

"How may I help you guys?"

"We just wanted to ask you a few questions about the days leading up to the bombing and anything you might've noticed," Minka told him.

"I appreciate your efforts, but I'm afraid I can't help you much. Ever since that night, I've combed through my memory for any warning signs, other than the general unrest in the city, but I can't put my finger on anything."

"Have you been involved in any personal disputes, sir?" Renee asked.

"None besides the ones the job demands. Why?"

Renee squared her shoulders. "The explosives that caused the blast are believed to have been in your office."

His eyes widened. "Detectives, I had no idea. Please, believe that. I love what I do, and I love this city. I would never do or aid in anything that would endanger either one of them."

"Who else has access to your office?" Minka questioned.

"Anyone, really. I don't keep the door locked. I usually just store my valuables in the file cabinet and lock that."

"Does your brother-in-law go in there much?" Renee asked.

"Tyler? Please don't tell me you suspect he was involved in this."

"We don't know," Renee said. "What we do know is he landed on our radar because his truck appeared to be the one carrying a bomb."

"Oh my," he responded, his dismay seeming to be genuine. "How can I tell my wife her little brother might be a terrorist?"

"It's still an ongoing investigation," Minka reminded him. She wondered how to continue, not wanting to incense her partner by giving away too much. "The vehicle just resembled his, and even so, the bomb in it was never detonated. It just seems suspicious that he was implicated, and now, you are, too. "

He put his hand to his mouth, visibly shaken. "I agree."

"Are you two on good terms?" Renee questioned.

He shrugged. "I guess. Despite us working in the same building, we don't interact often. I'm gone before he reports. Granted, we might cross paths more if he didn't have such trouble with punctuality."

Minka zeroed in on his awareness of Gill's tardy tendencies, but she didn't address it. "May we assume you helped him land the job?"

He nodded, wearing his regret. "I felt pity for him because of his dire straits, but he didn't appreciate it much. He's done nothing but criticize the place and does the bare minimum to keep his position. I've made it clear that I'm not accountable for his actions and that they're not under any obligations to keep him on-board for my sake."

"What complaints did he voice against his work?" Minka asked.

"The usual. Hated the hours, the wages, and his coworkers."

Renee's eyes glistened with intrigue. "Anything in particular about the courthouse?"

Judge Nichols didn't seize the opportunity to capitalize on her misgivings. "Not that I'm aware of. To tell you the truth, I don't think Tyler has enough motivation to stage something this elaborate."

His words allayed her suspicions of him framing his brother-in-law, but Minka had to determine his alibi. "Where were you that night?"

"At my son's eighth grade basketball game."

She made a mental note to verify that. "Do you think anybody else had it out for you or maybe wanted to send you a message?"

He frowned. "I can't say. I deal with a lot of bad people, and it wouldn't be hard to imagine one of them wanting revenge."

****

On the ride back from the judge's house, Minka and Renee went back and forth about the case, chatting with more ease than they'd shared all week. Renee ran through the details of each case she'd been involved in that Judge Nichols presided over and speculated which parties might have the means to pull off the bombing. Like he'd deduced, however, every instance included characters who would likely be after vengeance and unafraid of going to great lengths to get it.

To assist them in their investigation, the judge gave them the files he had at home on many of his past deliberations. With three boxes full, Minka and Renee split them when they returned to the precinct. Before she dug into her stack, Minka browsed the Internet to check into the middle school basketball games in the area that took place Sunday night. Her search uncovered three contests, all of which were suspended in the third quarter because of the bombing. Nonetheless, the judge's son played in one, and Nichols's wife posted a picture on social media, featuring the three of them together before tip-off.

With her skeptical mind appeased, Minka started her review of the files, which provided her with a glimpse into how much the city's crime rate had risen over the past five years. While she'd been coloring and playing dolls with her little girl, more drug deals, robberies, and murders ripped through Orlando than ever before in the city's history.

An hour into her browsing, she recalled why she used to vow never to take a job on the other side of law enforcement: the work bored her to death. Her eyelids drooped while she read over the documents and transcripts, and her brain shuffled around the facts of two or three different hearings. When she caught her slips, she poured over them again, slowing any progress she made to a halt.

To her surprise, her boredom distracted her enough to lose track of time. She didn't realize she needed to take a lunch break until she glanced across the desk and noted Renee's absence. She brushed off her irritation over her partner's failure to say anything and started to tuck away the report she'd just opened. Before she closed its folder, her weary eyes locked onto a familiar name, Kirk O'Connor.

The image of Gill's neighbor lit up in her mind as she read over the account of his trial, in which he stood accused of armed robbery at an outlet mall. He managed to clean out the cash at three stores and mugged two customers along his spree before security guards caught up to him. Though he had no priors, the judge sentenced him to a year in prison.

Months after his release now, a bomb was planted in the presiding judge's office, and his supposed best bud was framed in the crime. Minka mulled over the glaring connections while she ambled toward the break room. O'Connor vouched for Gill, claiming they were both working on Gill's car right before the bombing, but what if that was a well-devised cover for O'Connor? Could he, in fact, have done something to impede his friend from getting to the courthouse so that he could implicate him and tighten up his own alibi? Then again, would he have enough time to engineer the blast after waylaying Gill?

Lost in contemplation, Gus's voice startled her as she passed his office. He'd been busy all morning, so they didn't have the opportunity to brief him on their visit with Nichols.

After she finished relating the details of the unproductive interview, he asked, "Did Nichols have an alibi for the night of the bombing?"

"Yep. He was at his son's basketball game."

"At least you ruled that out."

With the clock ticking, she stepped toward the door to carry on with lunch, but she couldn't squander the chance to pick his brain about her quandary. "Speaking of alibis, I've stumbled across an interesting link between Gill's neighbor and the judge. Nichols handed over a bunch of his cases, and O'Connor was a defendant in an armed robbery two years ago. Nichols sentenced him to a year in prison. O'Connor says he was helping Gill with his car that night, which was Gill's excuse for being late to work, but I'm wondering if there could be more at play here."

"I can't say I'm shocked he and Gill would be friends, but given Gill's relation to Nichols, I'm curious how the sentence impacted their bond."

"So am I," she said. "Would I have your approval to contact him again and feel him out about it?"

"As long as you loop in your partner on it."

She rolled her eyes. "My partner didn't even give me a heads-up that it was time for lunch, which I guess I'd better get to."

Minka paced over to the door, but incoming Lola cut off her path. The friends hugged.

"Hello, Detective," Lola greeted with a grin. "You didn't get much time to settle in, did you?"

Minka shook her head. "I'm starting to get a complex about drawing the blockbuster crimes to me."

"As my husband can attest, they strike without any care about who has to unravel what they did."

"Unfortunately," Minka agreed. "I wish I could visit, but I have to scarf down some lunch. I hope we can get back to the chat that the bombing interrupted the other night."

Lola winked and slipped a sonogram out of her purse. "Well, I won't hold you up for long, but here's our first picture of the little one. I had my checkup today, and the doctor says we're right on track for thirteen weeks. I'm due in the middle of June."

"I'll bet Ryan's thrilled," Minka replied.

"Actually, he keeps hoping some apple seeds sprouted in my belly, and he'll get a pie out of this," she reported, making Gus and Minka chuckle. When the levity passed, she leveled a caring gaze at Minka. "I was really hoping we could go through all of the cravings and morning sickness together this time."

"Yeah, me, too. It's probably for the best, though. This way, we can trade kids when we're in the delivery room, instead of being side-by-side, with them playing in the corner with bedpans."

The couple laughed, and the concern in Lola's eyes dissipated. She padded over to her husband and grasped his hand. "That's right. I'm sure your time will come. Gus and I discussed it for years, and now it just feels perfect all around. You guys will get there, too."

Minka observed Gus straighten his posture, and his throat contracted in a hard swallow. Between that and Lola's blissful remarks, she suddenly made a troubling realization.

He hadn't told his wife that his job was in jeopardy.

As Minka excused herself and headed to her overdue lunch, she digested the turn of events, strengthening her resolution to do her part to save Gus's career.

****

After lunch, Minka informed Renee about Kirk O'Connor's history with Judge Nichols. She agreed the correlation was brow-raising and supported her view that they should interview him again. Thus, Minka called him and arranged a meeting at the precinct later in the afternoon.

The detectives and O'Connor sat down at the table,

and Minka began the questioning on a friendly note. "Nice to see you again, Mr. O'Connor."

"Is Tyler still in trouble?"

"No, but we'd still like to get some insight into your relationship," Minka stated. "How long have you known Tyler?"

"A few years. We met at a bar and were in similar boats, you could say. His family was disappointed in him, and the same went for me with my ex-wife. Two miserable souls bonding over failure and whiskey."

Sounds like a lyric in a country song. Minka took advantage of his reference to Gill's family. "His family must not have given up all hope on him for his brother-in-law to land him a job."

O'Connor grunted. "That was just his way of keeping him under his thumb. Nichols had the whole security team basically spying on him. Tyler's wanted out of it for a long time."

"Do you suppose he might've been involved in the bombing because of that? Maybe he wanted payback?" Renee questioned.

"No, it's not possible. I told you we were trying to fix his ignition that night."

Minka dropped the subject of Tyler for now and tiptoed closer to their ultimate destination. "Speaking of Judge Nichols, we happened to notice that he presided over your armed robbery trial, which ended in your jail sentence. Is that the reason behind your animosity toward him?"

"How would you like it?"

She deflected his question. "Did any of your negative feelings for him affect your view of Tyler?"

"Of course not. He had my back all along."

"Were you expecting preferential treatment because of that?" Renee asked.

"No. In fact, Tyler and I both expected our friendship to be my undoing."

"So, you believed Nichols convicted you because he had it out for you?" Minka replied.

He folded his arms. "I don't think he was truly unbiased."

"I'll bet that really upset you," Renee said.

"You'd better believe it did!"

Leaning forward in her chair, Minka cut to the chase. "Did it upset you enough to harm—or threaten to harm—the judge?"

O'Connor's bitter glower yielded to his alarm, his mouth agape. "What? Why is this starting to feel like an inquisition?"

"With Tyler's position on the security crew, you both would've had unique access to exact revenge on Nichols right under his nose," Renee stated. "Perhaps even the kind of revenge that explodes."

O'Connor shook his head. "Oh, I see. Since we were together, you're trying to put it on both of us. Well, he's not a terrorist, and neither am I. He and I could be called a lot of things, but that isn't one of them."

"Then, can you tell us where you were Sunday night, after you left his place?" Minka asked.

"Dropping off my kids at my ex's house. They stayed with me for the weekend, per our custody arrangement. And trust me, you don't have to worry about her lying for me."

The interview concluded abruptly, with O'Connor rising to his feet and heading out of the room. Minka shrugged her shoulders at her partner, who sauntered out of the room in a similar manner. Before he could exit the building, Minka hustled up to him to get his ex's phone number. He rattled it off, so she placed the call the instant she retreated to her desk. The woman armed her with a myriad of other counts against him, but in regard to the bombing, she substantiated his alibi.

With that awkward conversation behind her, she picked up a new file from the box Judge Nichols gave them, albeit with a jaded spirit. Nonetheless, she endeavored to keep both an objective and shrewd eye. The ones she selected happened to be fairly high-profile in the local area, so she recognized most of them from the news. The judge carried a heavy load in recent years, as it seemed he'd handled all of the major crimes in the city. The pool of potential suspects did anything but shrink.

Even so, nothing imperative struck her in the first folder she paged through. The next one, however, aroused her intrigue. The case surrounded a disgraced former football player, Braiden Fitz, who wore number twenty-five during his career—reminding her of Collector25, the person asking for the blueprints online. Fitz was accused of beating up his agent after a business deal flopped. Because of two other battery charges, in which judges served him minimal penalties, Nichols sentenced him to fifteen years.

Unable to ignore the irony, Minka slid the folder over to Renee, despite being well aware she may shoot it down as a possibility. She decided to adjust her methods, taking a more casual approach.

"Here's an interesting twenty-five correlation."

Renee's skeptical frown faded as she read it. "A

sentence like that doesn't win you any friends with the defendant's side, especially when the defendant expects a slap on the wrist. Prisoners have been known to seek revenge against the person who put them there, even from behind bars."

Minka glanced at her watch, which read four o'clock. "Visitation hours ended at three."

"I'm sure the warden would make an exception for a suspected bomber," Renee replied.

Chapter Four

Of all the duties entailed with law enforcement, Minka least enjoyed visiting a prison. Though a few of her own collars were now housed there, sorrow consumed her over the many tragic stories that lay behind the bars. Every inmate had someone who cared about them, whether they appreciated it or not, and they had a chance to lead better lives—again whether they appreciated it or not.

The two detectives explained their business to the warden, who permitted them entry. He led them through the community room, where Minka half-expected to witness brawls and such. Instead, the room hosted a full Pilates class. A drastic contrast to the convicts' former lifestyles, she ogled at the scene of these burly, tattooed men stretching in such docile poses. A grimace from one of the participants, however, reminded her of the environment.

The warden approached Fitz and after pointing out the detectives, cuffed his wrists, following protocol. The prisoner complied, and they headed to the nearby interrogation room. The detectives sat across from him, and Renee began the conversation in her usual snarky tone. "Looks like institutionalism agrees with you, Fitz."

"I'm trying to make the best of my circumstances, Detective."

Renee rolled her eyes. "So are you the convicts' official spokesman now? You must've hired a new agent."

Disagreeing with her partner's methods yet again, Minka intervened, "We won't take much of your time—"

"Even though you have plenty of it," Renee said.

Not faltering, Minka continued, "We were just curious about your feelings on the courthouse bombing."

"I'm glad no one was hurt too badly," he told them, his cadence mild.

Renee grunted, mocking him. "Sounds like someone's been taking acting lessons for his post-prison comeback."

He lost his calm countenance, with his eyes widening in alarm and his posture straightening with tension. He shifted his gaze between them. "You think I'm lying? Do you suspect me of being involved? Is that why you're here?"

"You have to admit, the place wasn't too kind to you," Minka stated. "Plus, the bomb was planted in Judge Nichols's office. You can't tell us you have the fondest of feelings toward him."

"That's exactly what I'll tell you," he said. "I owe that man everything. If not for him, I'd just be an entitled jerk who's hopped up on steroids and furious all the time. This gave me a wake-up call. I'm not the same guy. For the first time in my kid's life, she's proud of me, and so is her mom. We're nearly back together, in fact."

Renee spread out her arms in disdain. "The all-American dream."

Fitz dropped his gaze but maintained his innocence. "I realize I was a monster, and I understand why you guys don't trust me, but you have to. I even wrote Nichols a letter a few months ago to thank him for being so tough on me. Ask him."

"How do we know you weren't just buttering him up before you threatened his life?" Minka asked.

He glanced down at the cuffs locked to the table, his expression somber. "Because I've put my family through enough. My little girl's already known as the daughter of the tight end with the hot temper. Why would I add terrorist to that?"

"To give her street cred," Renee suggested.

Not giving up, Fitz pled his case further. "Look, I'm aware that it's hard to believe someone like me could change, but I have. After a lot of therapy and—I'm not ashamed to admit—some medication, this is truly who I am now."

****

After the detectives wrapped up their conversation with Braiden Fitz, they talked with the warden, his therapist, and Judge Nichols, as he'd suggested. All three confirmed his claims, with the judge showing them the letter to prove it. According to both the warden and his doctor, he had changed significantly since his arrival and now had a regular medication regime. As a last resort, they checked his visitors and phone records to determine if he'd been in contact with any unscrupulous characters, but nothing raised a flag.

On her way home, Minka sighed, discouraged by the latest dead end. Nonetheless, she kept in mind how satisfying it was to witness such a transformation in a felon. So often, everyone overlooked the reformatory part of prison, given how few took the chance to allow the system to rehabilitate them. Not many with Braiden Fitz's reputation would make the effort to change and recapture a semblance of a bright future. Though it did nothing to further the case, she deemed it a much-needed win for law enforcement.

Once she arrived at the house, she did her best to set work aside to focus on family. Ironically, they were focused on her work, immersed in a mystery board game on the living room floor.

"What's this?" she asked since Caela had never played it before.

Her daughter beamed. "It's a detective game. It's a lot of fun!"

Wes stood up to kiss her. "She heard Mommy mentioned on the news and asked what you do at work, so I figured this would be a good way to show her."

Picking up the box, Minka decided to have some fun of her own. " 'Ages eight and up'—Caela, do you think Daddy's mature enough to play this?"

Wes smacked her behind, as the little girl replied, "Nah, that's why I like playing with him. I like to win."

Her father tackled her to the ground and proceeded to tickle her. Shaking her head, Minka headed into the kitchen to fix dinner. While she finished up the chili, she'd thrown in the slow cooker that morning, she kept her ear tuned to the father-daughter antics.

"I think it was Mrs. Swan with the pipe in the game room," Caela made her accusation.

"It couldn't have been. She doesn't smoke."

Having spotted that he'd circled the suspect on his note, Minka stuck her head through the door and rebuked, "Daddy!"

"But I was so close," he whined.

As Caela crowed over the victory, he scooped her up and carried her out the back door. They chased each other around the yard as Minka made dinner. For most of the evening, she managed to relax and enjoy her family, casting her difficult week out of her thoughts. Caela wanted to demonstrate an art project she did at school, which became a glittery mess. It ended with the girl looking like a victim of a glitter explosion, forcing her mother to corral her into the bathroom. By the time Caela made it into the tub, Minka sparkled all over as well.

After bathing her and putting her to bed, Minka returned to the living room to vacuum up the sparkles on the carpet. She gave the rest of the room a touch-up, which led her to the stack of Judge Nichols's case files she'd carted home. In light of her long day, she hated to spend her hours before bed pouring over them, but she concluded that without a solid lead elsewhere, she should give it some attention.

During her review, her heart sank again at the evil that prevailed in the world, and a despondent sigh escaped her mouth.

Wes peered at her from across the couch. "Hard day with Detective Hart?"

"Well, yes, but I'm over that. I'm just remembering how dark this job is. I mean, I used to love it, even live for it. It gave me purpose and fulfillment, and I really missed it when I was home with Caela. Good grief, I watched cop shows while I nursed her."

"No wonder some of her first words were 'It's not mine!' " Wes joked.

Minka laughed, before her somberness returned.

"Here, I finally make my big comeback, and I'm starting to feel like everything I craved and dreamed about isn't what I really want anymore. My priorities and aspirations have completely shifted. Now that I've experienced what it's like to wake up every morning on the bright side of life, I don't feel that need to spend my day seeking out the dark side."

Wes took her in his arms. "I get it, babe. While I've always admired what you guys do, I've never wanted it for me."

"Never?" She raised a brow, calling out his one crack at crime-fighting—which ended in him landing on the mob's hit list.

He ignored her taunting. "The point is, I had a feeling you'd go through a culture shock in going from fairies and princesses to muggers and now terrorists."

"Why didn't you stop me, then?"

"Because you genuinely want to help people; that's why you joined the force. You know it as well as I do. Even on tough cases like this, you understand that there wouldn't be any bright side if you weren't out there trying to protect others. And I believe that's what you're going to do." He stroked her hair for a moment before he drew back his hand and spread it out in front of her face to display the residual glitter he inherited. "See, you're emitting that bright side without even realizing it."

Minka giggled and gave him a lingering kiss, dropping the file in her hand to allow her husband to preoccupy her.

****

The next morning, Minka awoke before Wes or Caela, so she took advantage of her unhurried start by taking a refreshing warm shower. After she finished, she tiptoed into the living room and switched on the morning news. She'd avoided it all week, not wanting to let the bombing dominate her home life or overexpose Caela to it. Alone, however, she could tolerate it and decided she should get a feel for how the community was reacting.

The moment she tuned in, the headline reading, *Courthouse Bombing: Terrorist Still at Large* stretched across the screen. The same images and information replayed as she assumed it had every day before the station aired a new clip of Chief Friedman's latest press conference.

He stood at his podium for the discourse. "This has been a tragic week for the city and the Orlando Police Department. Naturally, the public wants answers about the state of our investigation, so after days of fielding your questions, I'm going to tell you the truth. As the Chief of Police, I feel the public deserves to know that internal mismanagement has contributed to our lack of results in this case. The department has pursued a few bogus leads, causing several of our supposed best investigators to spend valuable time on worthless endeavors.

"It's a source of great frustration, and I hate to be the one to report this dysfunction. For the sake of safety of Orlando's fine people, I consider it my duty to paint a realistic picture of what we're facing here. At the same time, I'm vowing to see to it that these matters are corrected and to apprehend whoever's responsible for the attack on our city, no matter the cost."

Minka groaned and powered off the television, sorry she ever flipped to it. Her husband's voice from behind the couch startled her. "That whole dog and pony show was about him. Deep down, he knows you'll catch the jerk, and he's just positioning himself to take the victory. He's nothing more than a people-pleaser. My guess is he's gearing up for a political campaign or a spot on one of those reality series for washed-up celebrities."

Minka couldn't help but laugh at her husband's prediction. She agreed with his logic—at least up until the last sentence. Like Gus had told her days before, Friedman had to answer to people, too, and was out to save his own reputation first and foremost. Still, she had a difficult time focusing on much of anything except his words. She worried about the city, her job, and her friends, fortifying her resolve to crack the case—and the chief's ego in the process.

As much as it pained her, she backed up the segment and listened to the recap again, combing through the facts for anything she missed. The reporter called attention to the fortunate yet puzzling timing of the incident, and her brain locked in on that. They'd assumed the culprit chose the late hour because he wanted to send a message more than anything. Now, it almost seemed like a foolish assumption, especially considering the motive they suspected. Anyone, primarily with a record, who had it out for Judge Nichols would've acted when he was around. Felons didn't have the custom of being subtle. Thus, if the target were a particular individual, it'd only make sense to strike when he or she was there.

And the only ones present were the security guards.

What if that was where they'd gone wrong? Should they have been investigating the guards' lives, instead of focusing on the judge's? After all, the bomber knew what Gill used to drive, suggesting that he had some personal connection. What if that wasn't all the insight he had?

On a whim, she texted Cael to learn if he had any updates on Chet Wagner, the guard who was hospitalized after the blast. He divulged that the man was released from the ICU to the main floor and had agreed to answer more of their questions if needed. When she asked him if he and Declan minded if they followed-up, he gave her the go-ahead. She worried Renee wouldn't be so cooperative to the notion right at the start of the morning, but she didn't offer any push-back. On the contrary, she suggested she swing by so they could ride together to the hospital.

Just the same, her mood could chill an icebox when she entered the living room.

"Hi, Aunt Renee!" Caela adopted the nickname without Minka's knowledge or endorsement.

The detective didn't seem fond of it, either. "You can call me Detective Hart."

Minka put on her businesswoman exterior. She told Renee she needed to escort Caela to the bus, and with reluctance, she offered for her to wait in the living room. To her relief, her partner said she'd return to her car and catch up on some calls. As they exited the house, Camille scurried across the lawn, with her pace making it clear that she longed for a scoop.

She embraced Minka. "There's the working girl. I'm glad to see you're still taking some time with this sweet little girl."

Caela gave Camille the hug she requested but didn't linger in the embrace. "Sorry we can't talk,"

Minka told her between gritted teeth. "Duty calls."

"Yes, I'd imagine." Camille trailed behind them and couldn't resist engaging Renee in conversation. "I don't believe we've met before."

"I'm Minka's partner, Renee Hart," she said, irritating Minka in light of how she'd treated innocent Caela.

Camille shook her hand. "Excuse my dirty fingers. I'm planting my okra. If I have a good crop, I'll fry some and have you and Wes over, Minka. My crop didn't do well last year."

Renee's eyes lit up unlike what Minka had witnessed before. "Mine didn't, either."

While the thought of the vegetable made Minka cringe, the two women chatted at length on it, still carrying on about it by the time she returned from the bus stop. They exchanged stories, tricks, and eventually, phone numbers. After they finished, Minka realized why she and Renee couldn't see eye-to-eye— she was Camille with a badge.

On the bright side, Renee's chat with Camille warmed up her frosty demeanor, making it easier to deal with her. Minka didn't attempt to understand it but appreciated the thaw for however long it lasted. She related her theory about analyzing the guards' part in this, which revived Renee's fixation with Gill and improved her mood further. Still on the fence about him, Minka cringed over her odd delight, but she needed to acknowledge every possibility.

Once they parked at the hospital, they followed the receptionist's directions to Wagner's room, located in the center's burn unit. The guard sat upright on his bed, seeming alert as he watched television. Bandages covered part of his face and both hands, and the exposed skin on his arm had a red cast to it.

They swapped introductions with him and his grown daughter, Mackenzie, whose two-year-old son, Henry, drove toy cars over his grandpa's blanket. Mackenzie lured him out to the cafeteria so the detectives could talk to Wagner without Henry's tiny ears privy to the account. As the naive tot waved to his injured grandfather, Minka's heart ached over what the children of Orlando had to witness that week.

She snapped out of her sentimentality and centered her focus on the questioning.

Renee took the lead. "What do you recall from the night of the blast?"

"Nothing unusual. I arrived a few minutes early for my shift, as I always shoot for, and I made coffee for the rest of the crew. We visited while we waited to clock in and split up to our respective posts after that."

"You didn't notice any disturbances or peculiarities in the hour before the explosion?" Minka asked.

"None that I remember right now. As I told your colleagues, I can't extract anything from the moment of the blast. I was walking down a hallway, then I was here, with nothing in between."

"Your coworker, Tyler Gill, showed up late," Renee said. "Did you interact with him at all after he arrived?"

"Only over the intercom. When I realized he still hadn't come, I started toward his zone and paged him along the way. He finally responded when I approached the corridor, so I circled back to mine. I don't recall making it back, so I suppose that's when everything happened."

Renee lifted a suspicious brow over at her partner. Minka agreed Gill's timing seemed a bit too coincidental, but the questions surrounding his truck still made her hesitant to jump to conclusions.

"We've heard he didn't enjoy the job. Do you know any particular reason why?" Minka inquired.

Wagner shook his head. "As far as I could tell, he just didn't want to work. He's tried filing a couple of worker's comp claims, but he can never make a convincing case. The review board can sort out when you break your arm on the job versus in a bar fight."

"Did he dislike you personally?" Renee asked.

Wagner shrugged. "Maybe. He treated me okay, but I have written him up on occasion. That didn't win me his favor, as you'd imagine."

Renee cleared her throat and shifted her weight, signaling she'd gleaned as much as she needed. Minka, however, didn't want to conclude the discussion just yet. "How long have you worked at the courthouse?"

"Four years. I took the position after I retired from the asphalt plant to supplement my pension."

"Has anybody other than Gill seemed to resent the job?" Minka asked.

He paused, appearing contemplative. "We've had a lot of turnovers since I was hired. Besides my supervisor, I'm the only one who's been there for two consecutive years. Everyone just sees it as an easy job to go to when you're desperate. That said, they usually leave on amiable terms."

With her theory losing air, Minka clung to hope that it wouldn't deflate completely. "No personal beefs?"

He started to give a denial, but his eyes soon shone

with awareness. "Silas Everett worked there for only a few months last summer before getting the boot. He took incompetence to a whole new level, which is saying something for our team. On the occasions he actually reported, something would always disappear after his shift. Since he could sneak in and delete the surveillance footage, nobody could catch him, so we all landed in the hot seat. He kept claiming he was smoking in his car when we couldn't account for him, but he didn't fool us. We confronted him after the boss launched an investigation, and he begged us to cover for him. I couldn't let someone else pay for his deception, though."

"It wouldn't be difficult to believe, then, that he'd find some pleasure in harming you all at once, would it?" Minka replied.

"No, I guess it wouldn't."

****

As they traveled from the hospital, Minka used her phone to run a search on Silas Everett. In the past year, he'd moved five times, and she assumed it was due to his inability to hold down a job. She browsed through his social media, where he posted an array of rants about his workplaces, both before and after they terminated his employment. She deduced he lost his latest position at a gas station the previous week.

She related a few of her discoveries to her partner as Renee drove. "He seems like a very hostile person."

"Social media amplifies that in people. Take that Limburg kid as an example."

Minka agreed, but she didn't appreciate her tone. Renee downplayed every remark Minka voiced about Everett, making it clear she didn't deem him a credible suspect. She manifested such optimism when they discussed Gill, but her confidence faded away once Wagner mentioned Everett. Minka still sensed she liked Gill taking the blame, but she couldn't fathom why.

After her comment about social media, Minka opted to stop giving her a running commentary. When she spotted a slam to the courthouse, however, she couldn't suppress her misgivings. "Listen to what he wrote after the courthouse fired him: 'The court of public opinion never ceases to triumph above all. Can't understand what I ever did to that jury. One of these days, I'll blow up the whole box.' " She glanced at her partner. "We can't overlook this."

Renee sighed, before nodding. "You're right. I'm sorry if I've been hasty to put this on Gill. The city's unrest—not to mention Friedman's outburst last night—makes me anxious to nail down a culprit. I realize we need to be sure it's the right one."

"I can relate. A week ago, I expected learning how to use the new database would be my biggest hurdle the first few days. I would've never guessed I'd be investigating an attack of this magnitude, much less with the Chief of Police inciting the public against us."

Renee snickered, the foreign sound startling Minka's ears. "I hear you. I agree that we should look into Everett, but I just can't get Wagner's experience with Gill out of my head. I mean, he arrived minutes before the bomb detonated, without enough time to make it to his corridor, where the bomb just so happened to go off. If that's a coincidence, I ought to allow my husband to start playing the lottery again. Maybe Gill and Everett hatched the scheme together."

Minka pondered the possibility but soon stumbled

on a snag. "If so, why would they rig up a truck to resemble Gill's? They'd have to be pretty wasted not to understand how it would implicate him."

"They might've expected the blast to destroy it altogether. They probably wanted it to blend in when they parked it and didn't anticipate us to figure out which vehicle carried the explosives."

"But in that case, why did Gill scrap his truck earlier in the week?" Minka replied.

"He just claimed to get rid of it. I'm telling you he coerced the junkman to confirm it. Guys like that don't have any scruples."

Minka despised the bold-faced stereotype, but she held her tongue. At the precinct, the two learned his latest address and hurried to it, only to discover his landlord already evicted him. After that setback, they scoured his public records for clues into his whereabouts. Without a current employer or family nearby, however, they couldn't nail down anything conclusive.

Amid the series of disappointments, Minka received a text from Wes, telling her an unexpected meeting arose at work. Since her mother-in-law wasn't available to pick up Caela either, Minka took Lola up on her offer from the other day and arranged to drop by for her daughter on the way home. Lola agreed without hesitation and even invited the whole family over for pizza.

Though delayed by a tip on a case Renee had before the bombing, Minka still beat her husband to the Channings'. Upon parking her crossover, she noted the *For Sale* sign in the yard. Given Gus's precarious job situation, she couldn't decide whether to interpret their desire to move as a positive or negative development.

She chose to pretend she didn't notice it and proceeded inside. Lola wandered out of the kitchen and embraced Minka. They strolled into the living room, where the collage of family photos had been stripped from the wall and sat in a box below their usual place.

Minka nodded in that direction. "Making room for the new baby photos already?"

"No, those will hopefully go up in the new house. We met with our realtor yesterday, and she suggested I put away all of our personal touches to attract buyers. I'm going to replace them with some cheap paintings I bought at the flea market this morning."

"With how often my parents moved, Mom didn't bother hanging up our pictures after a certain point. Wes asked me if we believed in cameras the first time we visited their house," Minka replied, making them chuckle. "How long ago did you decide to sell?"

"We started throwing around the idea when we learned I was pregnant, but we didn't get serious about it till a couple of weeks ago. The perfect place just popped up on the market, but for some reason, Gus won't bid on it yet. It's in our price range with four bedrooms, so the kids would each have their own, and we'd have one for guests. Plus, it's walking distance from the school. But you know my husband. Always hunting for a better buy."

Minka understood Gus's reluctance, but she didn't dare intrude on another couple's disagreement. Instead, she resorted to humor. "Maybe he doesn't want a guest room so readily available. After living with my brother for a month, I have that aversion, too."

"He did lock my folks out of the house on their last

visit, by accident, so he says," Lola admitted with a giggle.

"Where is he, anyhow?" Minka asked.

"In his office. He's been fielding calls all week, as you can probably relate. You can go check on him if you want to while I order the pizza."

"I will. Wes says he's on his way now."

After they deliberated on the pie's toppings, Minka meandered toward the back of the home. The door to the study stood open, but she waited to make sure he wasn't on the phone. A few silent seconds elapsed, so she tapped on the mahogany entry to announce her arrival. He barely tore his attention from his computer screen.

"Fantasy baseball draft already?" she teased.

"Huh? No, I'm taking a practice captains' exam. The real one's tomorrow."

"Tomorrow? Don't you think that's a little soon? You've been studying for what? Two days?"

"Hardly, and it shows. This is my third try today, and I haven't scored over sixty-five percent yet. But if I don't take it this week, there isn't another chance for two months, and I'm afraid that'll be too late."

Minka worried it wouldn't be enough, as it was. The chief was threatening him because of the case, not because of his rank. She doubted any title would save him as long as the bomber remained unpunished. Even so, she did her best to be encouraging. "I'm sure you'll pass. 'Captain Channing' just sounds too perfect."

"I like to think so," he replied.

She hated to lower the mood, but she couldn't ignore the chief's biting rhetoric for any longer. "Did you see it?"

"You mean my death sentence? Why do you think I'm in here, instead of helping my pregnant wife pack up a house we'll lose anyway if I get fired?"

As much as she wanted to boost his despondent spirits, her worry over Lola's ignorance overthrew her oath of silence. "I gather you haven't told her anything."

"I couldn't. Not this week, at least. We had the ultrasound and the open houses to go to, and I didn't want to spoil it for her."

"But the longer you wait, the worse it'll be."

"I appreciate your concern, but just give me a fighting chance to straighten this out on my own."

A variety of rebuttals flooded her throat, but she caught them. As she trotted out of the room, she reflected again on the chance he extended her in Atlanta…

After she ended her conversation with Detective Channing, Minka dug up all she could on Claire's ex, Justin Harris. She didn't think much time had passed since she last ran into Claire leaving for their date, but he was already engaged to a different girl. Minka surmised it was the possessive woman Detective Channing mentioned as she scoured their wedding website. In all of their photos, Justin's fiancée clung to him, and the page that shared their love story boasted that their whirlwind romance began once they both realized they were with the wrong people.

Minka finished her shift and headed to the gym Justin owned. Given she couldn't claim to be on police business, she decided to pay for a workout session, reckoning she needed one, regardless. She didn't spot her target for the first part of her regiment, but he eventually emerged from his office. On the stair-climber, Minka didn't rush over to him, but she soon contrived a way to be discreet.

She carried a pair of dumbbells. "Excuse me, but do you have any thirties?"

"We should."

She followed him to the weight rack, where he retrieved some and handed them to her. She thanked him but wouldn't let him retreat right away. "I think I've met you at my building. Aren't you Claire Pennbrook's boyfriend?"

He winced. "Not anymore."

"Oh, I'm sorry. I live next door to her, but I've been worried about her lately because she hasn't been home in a couple of days. I'm sure you don't know anything about that."

"No, but I just saw her last week."

A nearby coworker of his swept past them and jabbed him in the side. "Much to Nadia's chagrin."

"Who's Nadia?" Minka questioned.

He blushed. "My fiancée. She just gets a little jealous. Plus, she has some jitters over our big day."

Minka crossed her arms. "Claire sensed somebody was following her. Do you think your bride might have anything to do with that?"

"Absolutely not. Nadia doesn't even drive."

Minka made a mental note to check out whether the girl had a driver's license or vehicle registered to her. "Did Claire act any differently than normal when you last spoke?"

"I mean, things have definitely changed from when we were dating, but she was fine, other than being stressed from her deadlines at work."

"She's a reporter, right?"

He nodded. "She writes whatever they assign her to, but she's trying her crack at exposés. From the impression she gave me, I'm guessing she's onto something big."

A trainer cut off the conversation, but once Minka returned to her bench, she texted Detective Channing to tell him she may have a lead.

Considering the leniency Gus offered her to explore Claire's disappearance, she reasoned she'd better give him room to navigate his challenges.

Chapter Five

On Friday, Renee surprised Minka by suggesting they dig some more into Silas Everett. This time, they investigated what he drove to track him. Like Gill, he owned several vehicles, with one being impounded because of a parking violation a couple of days earlier. Given they had little else to go on, they headed to the impound lot.

The manager led them to an SUV and reported that no one had inquired about it since they towed it. He allowed them to inspect the inside, so Renee combed through the front while Minka took the back cargo area. As soon as she swung open the hatch, a pungent odor wafted out. She noticed white powder blanketing the floor.

"Are you seeing this?" Minka asked.

"No, but I can smell it." Renee stepped back to survey the compartment. "It's too pungent to be coke."

"It smells sort of like ammonia," Minka said.

"That's it!" Renee declared. "It's ammonium nitrate fertilizer."

"A popular ingredient in making a bomb," Minka replied with conviction. "Everett is our guy."

They started snapping photos of the contents and informed the manager they'd have to seize the vehicle as evidence. Minka sent a couple to Gus, who immediately responded with a call.

"We found him!" Minka proclaimed the minute he answered. "The security guard we met with at the hospital mentioned a guy who was fired a few months ago, Silas Everett. We tracked down an SUV of his that was impounded a few days ago, and the back is filled with what we suspect to be ammonium nitrate. We're taking a sample and seizing the vehicle."

"Nice work, Minks. If it checks out, we'll release the information and Everett's picture to the press and put eyes out for him. In the meantime, I want you guys to dredge up all you can on him and narrow down where he could've bought that fertilizer. It's hard to find somebody to sell that stuff in large quantities for obvious reasons."

She agreed to the command, before a grin formed on her lips. "Make sure to call the chief."

"I'm already dialing."

After they ventured back to the precinct, Minka and Renee spent the next ninety minutes tracking down where ammonium nitrate could be purchased. As Gus had mentioned, many stores didn't sell it, especially in the amount Everett must've bought, and they should've reported such a purchase. None of the major stores carried it, and the smaller hardware shops that did told them they hadn't made any sales in the past two months. In every conversation they had, however, one business was always mentioned—Twyla's Feed Store.

Just a few blocks away, they didn't bother calling before they drove over, preferring a face-to-face meeting. The older building was nothing like what most people pictured of Orlando architecture. It looked rundown and carried a rural feel, uncommon to the downtown area. Then again, the animal feed and agricultural store didn't cater to city folk, despite its location.

Striding inside, the odor of the live farm animals—albeit small ones—took Minka by surprise. Her strong sense of smell always kept her out of the country life. Nobody manned the counter at the time, with a woman cleaning the chicks' pen. She gave them a warm greeting, displaying southern charm at its finest.

"Afternoon, ladies." She rose to her feet, shaking their hands. "I'm Lucy. I don't believe I've seen either one of you girls in here. New to the farm?"

"You could say that," Minka replied, beginning to hold her breath. "We're here on business, actually. I'm Detective Avery, and this is Detective Hart, and we're investigating the courthouse bombing."

"Oh, dear, bless your hearts. I don't care what that chief says, I'm certain you're all doing your best."

Minka nodded. "We are, and that's why we're here, Lucy. We were wondering if you sell ammonium nitrate."

"Of course. It yields great results. Very popular."

"You've had recent orders, then?" Minka asked.

"A few lately. It isn't our busiest season right now."

"Any big purchases?" Renee kept her on track.

"No, just a bag here and there."

The statement didn't surprise Minka, as the strategy would've kept the operation inconspicuous. She located a photo of Everett on her phone and showed it to her. "Do you recognize him?"

She shook her head. "I can ask around to see if my colleagues have interacted with him."

"May we have a record of your sales?"

She nodded, maintaining her cheery smile, until her eyes glinted with the sober epiphany. "Wait a minute. You don't think…" The woman backed up to lean on the nearby counter, the weight of the possibility seeming to drive her body.

"We're not clear on any details, ma'am. We're just collecting information," Renee told her.

"We appreciate your help," Minka added, touched by the woman's emotional reaction.

Lucy regained her balance and wandered behind the cash register. She typed something on her computer, before a page began printing. Tears still filled her eyes when she handed the sales report to Minka. "My family fled our home in Venezuela because of violent attacks like we saw here last weekend. To think that I might've aided in this kind of act…it sickens me."

Minka offered her a comforting handshake. "But you may help us catch whoever did it."

****

Back at the station, Minka and Renee studied the buyers on Lucy's list, but they didn't spot Everett's name. Several of the bags were purchased with cash, which prevented the store from needing further information. They suspected those were the ones used nefariously, but they couldn't form a solid conclusion.

Meanwhile, the lab confirmed the powder was fertilizer, so with some persuasion, the district attorney's office granted them a warrant to access his financials and phone records. Neither yielded much, as he hadn't made any outstanding withdrawals and seemed to be staying in the general area. They contacted his parents and sister who all lived in Arkansas, but they claimed they didn't have regular correspondence with him.

After they made five unsuccessful attempts to get ahold of him, they and Gus decided to spread word to the press, naming him a person of interest. While it served to placate Chief Friedman for the moment, the announcement made life at the precinct even more frenzied. The phones began ringing nonstop the instant they sent out the media release, with all outlets wanting the full story. Countless tips followed, but none netted anything useful. People just wanted to play a part in taking down the man responsible for the city's act of terror.

The madness spelled a long afternoon for Minka and Renee, as everyone wanted a comment from the case's lead detectives. Minka retreated home exhausted again, and like on Wednesday, she found Wes and Caela playing their detective board game on the coffee table. Her wily daughter now understood Wes's ploys in reasoning, and she joined him in his escapades.

Wes cleared his throat to make an accusation. "I'll say it's Mr. Brown with the hammer in the kitchen."

"No, Daddy, he has no reason to be in the kitchen; he doesn't cook."

Minka raced into the room to give her a high-five. "That's my girl!"

Wes gave his wife a grin as she kissed him and told him she'd heat up the leftover chili from Wednesday night. She continued to listen to their banter over suspects and reveled in the humor of the imagined alibis. Though her husband's kooky ways could—and did—land him in trouble at times, she loved the fun perspective he added to life.

The shenanigans made her mind drift back to the

case, and ironically, her husband's cunning logic led her to an unexpected revelation. Everett knew the courthouse's layout from working there, which, yes, would've made him the ideal candidate to devise the bombing. If he'd acted alone, however, why would he take on the Collector25 alias and elicit the blueprints? For that matter, judging by his living conditions, Minka doubted that he even had the substantial sum he offered in the first place. In his short time as an employee, he'd proven sneaky enough cover up his exploits; a scheme like this should've been relatively easy with just his crafty mind and experience.

It'd only stand to reason, then, that Everett didn't act alone. Chances were, in fact, he was more of the back-up plan, with another party in charge of the explosives inside the building. Everett's duties could've merely consisted of setting up Gill and detonating the bomb in the truck if anything went wrong. The real mastermind remained unknown.

After only half of her food was eaten, the breakthrough sapped Minka of her appetite. They'd made major strides that day, but now, their accomplishments didn't shine as brilliantly. Media outlets everywhere were painting Everett to be a terrorist when he might've just been the fall guy.

She didn't voice her doubts at the dinner table, allowing Caela to take the lead in their conversation. She realized the time would come when her daughter wouldn't reveal much about her day, so she cherished the girl's candor while she had it, even if her stories often ran together. Once they finished, Minka helped her with her homework and drew her a bath. In the mood to soak and play for a bit, Caela asked her mom to leave her alone.

Minka trotted out to the living room and checked her phone for any updates. Her revelation resurged in her mind, and she debated what she should do about it. Telling Renee would only wallop more misery onto her angst, but she hated to share it with Gus, either. He seemed more chipper than he had all week after they decided to alert the media, and she didn't want to rob him of that.

Wes glanced across the couch. "Any news about Everett?"

"Nope."

"I expected you to do cartwheels into the house when the report about him broke."

"Well, the mood really lightened after we released it, but the flood of phony tips stole some of our zeal," she told him.

"I'm sure you're close to a breakthrough."

"I'm afraid I've already made one but not the kind we're seeking." She proceeded to relate her theory about Everett being an accomplice to the actual bomber.

"But, babe, if his partner didn't detonate the bomb, he would've. He was ready to take on that role, if needed, and he should have to pay for that. Plus, he can lead you to whoever was in on it with him. There's no reason to feel guilty."

"I don't feel guilty on his behalf. I feel guilty on the department's. We named him the prime suspect, and we're going to look like fools when we have to confess that he isn't."

"He's the only piece of the puzzle you know for certain, so that makes him your prime suspect."

Minka's head pounded with frustration. "I agree, but I don't think the press will interpret it that way. More importantly, I'm afraid Chief Friedman won't, either. Just when I celebrated vindicating Gus, it'll probably end up being another nail in his coffin."

Wes sighed and paused for a moment. "Who says you have to clue anybody in on this? You could keep it under your hat until you detain Everett. Then, you could corner him about his accomplice. He'll tell you who he is, you'll be hailed as the hero, and Gus will be automatically promoted. How's that sound?"

"Sounds like the advice of a man who can't beat a kindergartener even at fake sleuthing!" Minka joked.

"Yeah, I guess crime-fighting's never been my strong suit." He winked, before narrowing the gap between them. "But I'm good at other things."

Just as he went to make his next move, Caela's voice drifted from the bathroom. "Mommy, I want to get out."

****

Raising her head to consult the clock, Minka groaned in disgust when she read four thirty. Consumed by the state of the case, she'd hardly slept all night. Though she'd poked fun at Wes's suggestion to keep quiet about her suspicions of Everett having a partner, the notion tempted her. Admitting their error in judgement would doubtlessly take center stage in the media, and locating Everett would become yesterday's news. Besides, maybe putting him on everyone's radar would lure his accomplice into slipping up out of pride.

But if nobody, except her, was searching for him, would it even matter? Worse yet, what if the city's hunt for Everett allowed the true bomber to escape unnoticed, if he hadn't already? The wrong move could put the city—if not the nation—in grave danger. After weighing out all of the uncertainties, Minka determined she couldn't take such a risk on her own.

Even so, her resolution wouldn't come without its anxieties. When she arrived at the precinct, everyone manifested a cheerful demeanor, despite having to report on a Saturday. The tip line continued to ring, and in spite of most of them being unsubstantiated, a strong sense of unity and hope prevailed. Needless to say, Minka hated to be the one to ruin the refreshing atmosphere she helped create.

Challenging her resolution even more, Gus made a one-of-a-kind entrance. Unusually late, the lieutenant set the station abuzz when he drove up in a charcoal sports car. Every guy in the building stormed up to the windows, and some, including Cael and Declan, dashed out to the parking lot to get up close and personal with the vehicle. After they gawked over it, they all marched in, and the rest of the men greeted Gus with chants of approval.

"It's only a rental, guys. Calm down." Despite the admonishment, his Cheshire grin revealed how much he ate up the attention.

Befuddled, Minka followed him into the office, noticing the new blond specks in his brown hair. "Have you lost your mind?"

"Oh, come on, Minks. My car's in the shop, so I just figured I'd have a little fun."

"You must have better insurance than we do. Last time mine was in for maintenance, they gave me a glorified golf cart."

He shrugged. "Well, I had to chip in a couple

hundred bucks, but I work hard."

"Did they throw in the hair dye, too?"

Her question seemed to puzzle him at first, but then he touched his head upon remembering his new hairdo. "No, this was Lola's. She bought it before we found out about the baby and decided not to use it, so I gave it a try. Dare I ask what you think?"

Given that she'd be squelching his good mood soon enough, she opted not to give him brutal honesty. "I'll get used to it."

"Well, Lola likes it, and with all due respect, that's what counts in my book. I guess yesterday just gave me this new lease on life, you know? I felt like everything I've built was about to collapse around me, and then suddenly, it all fell right back into place, better than ever. No wonder people who emerge from near-death experiences set out to do whatever they want. They realize how precious life is."

Though a sports car wouldn't be her way of celebrating life, Minka could relate to his feelings, having grown to appreciate hers more after nearly losing Wes years ago. His newfound optimism made her misgivings that much harder to confess. "Gus, about the case—"

"Hold that thought, Minks." He put his hand up, while he fixed his attention on his computer screen. From his posture and his intent expression, she deduced he received his exam results. He confirmed her suspicion when he sighed. "I didn't pass."

"I'm sorry."

He wore his disappointment, but he maintained a strong front. "Oh, well. I'm pretty sure Everett's bought me some time, at least. The chief even hinted at giving me a raise if we can find him. I'll just keep studying. Now, what were you saying about the case?"

His defeat drained her of willpower, and she couldn't go through with her plan. "We're going to do our best to track Everett down."

He winked. "I'm banking on it."

Exiting his office, Minka groaned inside, having accomplished nothing. She sank down into her seat and flipped through her notes from the previous day. She skimmed over the report about Silas Everett's SUV being impounded, given they'd hurried to the lot without paying much attention to the details of the incident. The officer who cited him recorded that he parked in the same fire lane on seven occasions over the past three months. Since he clearly visited the area on a regular basis, she ran a search on the address, which revealed it was a bargain souvenir shop.

She and Renee headed for it, and upon arriving, they parked in one of the legal spots. The building mirrored many of the others in town, painted vibrant colors that would make any kid on vacation beg their parents to stop and browse. In her eleven years of living in Orlando, she'd visited the majority for that very reason, with Caela always eager for a new princess outfit. She typically obliged her, preferring to buy the two-year-old merchandise rather than pay the exorbitant prices inside the attractions.

The man at the register attended to a customer when they strode inside, so they waited to approach him until he finished. Renee spoke up after the customer departed. "Sir, we're with the police department and would like it if you could give us some insight into one of your patrons."

"I'll try."

She showed him a picture of Everett. "This man is a person of interest in the courthouse bombing, and we just learned he's accrued several parking violations here. Do you recognize him?"

He dropped his gaze and took off his glasses to rub his eyes. "I'd hoped it was a misunderstanding, but yes, I know Silas. He stays in the apartment above the store from time to time. He worked for me one summer as a teen, and we hit it off. He's lived a rough life, and I always have a soft spot for him."

"Is he here now?" Minka asked.

The man shook his head. "He spent a few nights here this week, but he took off after the cops impounded his car. I kept telling him not to park there, but he wouldn't listen."

"Was he here the night of the bombing?" Minka replied.

"No, he arrived the next day. I even mentioned it, but he merely said it was a shame."

"What's he driving now?" Renee questioned.

"The rusty green pickup I gave him years ago. I'm sorry I didn't call in a tip. He lost his mother at a young age, and he never recovered. I just didn't want to betray him and add to his hardships."

"Unfortunately, others may suffer if we don't detain him," Renee replied.

He nodded. "I understand, and again, I apologize. I don't know where he's gone, but I'll tell you that, before he left, he asked to take some clothes and sunglasses. I deemed it peculiar, since he hasn't expressed interest in any of the merchandise in the past, but I didn't challenge him on it. Now, I wish I did."

Minka and Renee asked to inspect the apartment for anything he may have left behind, but the search didn't yield anything. The owner promised to inform them of any further contact he had with Everett.

Back in Renee's car, Minka sighed over another fruitless venture. "Now, our manhunt gets even more difficult, with Everett dressed as one of the thousands of other tourists in this city."

"I don't dare ask if it can get worse."

The instant the words escaped Renee's lips, the debate Minka grappled with all night resurfaced, and she couldn't repress it any longer. In an effort to win her partner's favor—or her tolerance, at the very least—she decided to go the casual route. "With so much madness, I almost forgot about the blueprints."

Renee didn't acknowledge the remark.

Minka rolled her eyes and paused a few moments before attempting to recreate her epiphany from the evening before without sounding canned. "Wait a minute: if Everett was behind the whole bombing, why would he need the blueprints? He was familiar with the building's layout."

That captured her partner's attention. "What are you saying?"

"I don't know. I just can't understand why a former employee would offer to pay thousands of dollars for information he didn't need. His financials don't indicate he even had that kind of money. Maybe he wasn't acting alone."

"Please, tell me you're kidding."

"I wish I were, but it sounds like a reasonable question, don't you think?"

"I suppose." She leaned back in her seat, her

expression showing a mix of frustration and puzzlement. "If he was working with someone, why would they even elicit the prints? Wouldn't you assume they chose to hire or conspire with him because of his history there?"

"Maybe they met him after they put the ad out, or maybe that's how they connected with him. A whole month passed between the request and the bombing. He could've just been a last-minute addition."

"Man, won't the press love this." Renee rubbed her temple. She paused for a moment, before she unwittingly started speaking Wes's language. "Why don't we keep this on the down-low for now? Let's focus on finding Everett, and then, we'll see what we can get out of him."

Minka didn't like the idea any more than she did the night before, but she restrained her protests. "Okay."

****

After checking Everett's financials again, Minka and Renee confirmed that he hadn't made any withdrawals for ten grand, nor did he ever possess such an amount. Since their last review, he'd made a withdrawal at an ATM on the north side of town. He used the machine several times before, so they combed through his past residences. He lived in the neighborhood with a woman the previous summer. Unable to accept the coincidence, the two wasted no time in heading her way.

The apartment complex was no palace, but Peta Lawson's door had a homey feel, with a colorful wreath of flowers and a matching welcome mat. The woman who greeted them exuded the same cheery aura, making it hard to imagine her being involved with a guy like Everett.

"How can I help you, Detectives?" Peta asked after inviting them inside.

"You may have seen on the news that we have a suspect, Silas Everett, in the courthouse bombing, and we noticed that he used to live here," Renee said. "We just wondered if you've connected with him recently?"

"No, we haven't had any contact since he moved. It was a tough breakup, but I couldn't believe it when his photo flashed on the news last night. We had our differences, but I never would've thought he'd be capable of this."

"Were you two together when he was working at the courthouse?" Minka asked.

"Yes. In fact, I dumped him because he was fired. Think what you will of me, but it was the third job he'd lost in a year. I was sick of it. I have a son, and he's enough to take care of. Plus, I didn't want him to follow Silas's example."

"So, your son isn't his child?" Renee asked.

"Thankfully, no."

Going back to Everett's employment history, Minka questioned, "Did he tell you why he was fired?"

"He blamed his coworkers, as he always does. I figured more lay behind it, though."

"Did he tell you his coworkers accused him of stealing?" Renee replied.

Peta nodded. "He denied it, but I had a feeling all along. He came home with all sorts of stuff he couldn't have afforded. When I asked him about it, he said his boss had given him a bonus, but I couldn't imagine that happening with all the work he missed."

"You obviously knew he disliked his job," Renee said.

"Oh, yeah. He'd complain day and night. Like I said, I didn't want that influence on my son anymore."

Right before the detectives concluded the discussion, an empty box of black hair dye in a nearby trash can caught Minka's attention. She glanced back at the woman's blonde locks and connected the dots. "You and your son live alone here now?"

"Yes."

"Do you think he'd like to meet us? A lot of kids usually get a kick out of meeting real, live cops." Her offer garnered a confused frown from her partner.

The unsuspecting mother grinned. "I'm sure he would."

The little boy—a towhead—appeared and shyly shook their hands. Their conversation didn't last long, as the seven-year-old remained focused on the video game on his tablet. Once he returned to his bedroom, Minka headed in for a landing. "Before we leave, could you tell us who used the black hair dye in your garbage?"

Peta didn't even peek toward the trash. "Just a friend."

"In the interest of national security, ma'am, we really need the name of that friend," Renee told her.

Her gaze fell to the floor, and she paused, her deliberation almost audible. "Silas Everett. He stopped over right before the alert broke, and he didn't tell me what he'd done. He just said he needed a fresh start and asked me to do his hair. I resisted at first, but he forked over two grand and swore he'd never bother us again, especially if I kept quiet about it."

Minka sensed her sincerity. "We won't allow him to bother you anymore. We need your help, though, and it may not be easy."

She hesitated, crossing her arms. A couple of moments later, she expelled a weary sigh. "I'll do whatever I can."

****

With Gus and the district attorney's consent, they arrested Peta, in hopes of luring Everett onto the grid. They claimed she refused to cooperate with the investigation and charged her with aiding and abetting in a crime—charges that would ultimately be dropped. Furthermore, they allowed her out on bail that wouldn't be collected, explained the situation to her boss, and guaranteed she'd retain custody of her son.

Before they released her, they asked her to place a call to the real man in question, in an effort to trace the call and get into his current state of mind. He didn't answer on the first two rings, making Minka believe he'd either pitched his phone or wouldn't pick up. Startled when his voice sounded through the speaker, she almost leapt in her seat.

"Don't buy into everything you hear, Peta," he said as soon as he answered.

"It doesn't matter what I hear or believe, Silas. You involved me by coming over and forcing me to give you a mini-makeover. The police consider me an accomplice in this now. They arrested me and said I might lose Aleck. If I'm taking the heat for this, I deserve the truth. Did you bomb the courthouse?"

A pregnant pause followed. "The more I tell you, the more they can squeeze out of you. All I can say is that I have an escape plan, but it hasn't fallen into place as swiftly as I was promised. When it does, I'll help you guys get out of this."

"But Sil—"

He terminated the call before Peta could protest further and seconds before they could lock onto his location. He never accused Peta of assisting the police, but Minka wondered if he suspected it and even understood how long he had until they busted him. Regardless, regret stung her for using Peta to this degree, given Everett's lack of consideration for her family's well-being.

Not to her surprise, they yielded nothing else from him for the rest of the day or the two after it, so they dropped the fake charges against Peta and released the burden from her. In the frustrating silence, Minka pondered what he meant when he referenced an escape plan. If he intended to make a break for another state or country, why wouldn't he do it while the city was hunting him? Sure, he dyed his hair, but that couldn't protect him for long. With no family or job in Orlando, why would he feel obliged to stick around?

He claimed he was waiting on things to fall into place, which piqued her curiosity more than anything. He risked his freedom every day he stayed in central Florida, so what would be worth that? She could only assume money, but from whom? With his face all over the news, he shouldn't expect anybody who owed him money to give it to him without calling the authorities. Even if he won the lottery, he'd be taking a chance just by claiming the ticket. Besides, did he really need the funds if he had two-thousand bucks in cash to pay Peta to dye his hair?

Everything pointed back to him having a partner. If

the other party was willing to pay for insider information, it'd make sense that he or she would compensate an accomplice for aiding the crime. Considering the time that had passed since the bombing, however, why wouldn't he have received the reward already? Did the plotter have more difficultly balancing a checkbook than committing terrorism?

Through all her speculating, Minka grappled with the decision to keep mum about the possibility of this being a two-man mission. The accomplice could be anywhere, convinced he's in the clear and contriving another attack. If he carried one out, she couldn't live with the fact that she may have been able to prevent it.

Nonetheless, she stuck to her resolve—or, more fittingly, Wes's and Renee's—and resisted her inclinations. The sight of Cael's car approaching the driveway Monday night tested her determination further. When he ducked into his backseat and lifted out Tyson, though, she surmised the visit didn't concern work.

He carried the screaming baby up to the doorstep and extended him to Minka. "Fix him."

She hoisted the baby up and asked him, "What's the matter with Daddy, sweetie?"

"Daddy's fed up," Cael grumbled. "Autumn's working late, and this guy cried all day at Mom and Dad's house. I've tried everything to comfort him: held him, rocked him, and burped him. I've been driving for over an hour, but he's only getting louder. I even called Autumn so he could hear her voice, and he just flipped."

"I can relate to that feeling." Minka snickered, before she inspected the tot's mouth and discerned the reason for his crankiness. "He has another couple of teeth breaking through down here. I have some peppermint I used for Caela. It'll numb up those gums before you know it."

"From colic to teething—a parent's dream!"

"You'll survive your baby," she said with a smile.

He sighed and collapsed on the couch. "Sometimes I wonder."

Digging the small jar out of the kitchen drawer, Minka took Tyson back into the living room. She dabbed some of the mint on his soft little gums, as Cael received a text. He soon let out a disgusted groan.

Since Tyson had just stopped crying, his irritation puzzled her. "What's wrong?"

He shook his head. "A new article just came out online about the investigation, and it's liable to derail the whole thing. The title alone will create chaos: *Low Prosecution Rate Leads to Bombing and Cover-Up.*"

"What?"

He cleared his throat and read aloud, "A photo posted online this afternoon has ignited a whirlwind of new conspiracy theories against the Orlando PD. Taken and posted by an unknown source, the snapshot, dated less than a week before the courthouse bombing, shows prime suspect Silas Everett and a mysterious person wearing a baseball cap. What's more, he or she appears to be wearing a police badge on his or her belt. It is, admittedly, blurred, and the supposed badge is too small to identify as one of the OPD's, but many say this is enough proof for them. The Chief of Police himself stated that the investigation had been mishandled, and this incriminating photo would explain why."

Minka continued to bounce her nephew as she

peered over Cael's shoulder. "Let me guess who uncovered this conspiracy—Finn Steward, Orlando PD's biggest fan."

"It's his typical garbage. A bunch of unnamed sources claim to know it all. According to them, there's been growing tension between us and the judicial system because of the dwindling convictions this past year. We finally reached our breaking point and hired Everett to unleash our vengeance. What a joke."

She bent down to study the photo. "It does look convincing."

"Sure, that's Everett, but how can you say that's one of ours? The badge is barely a speck. It could easily be mocked up."

She exhaled the breath she didn't realize she was holding and acknowledged he probably called it right. Still, the weight of her suspicions about Everett's possible accomplice sat on her chest like a bear. "While we're on the subject—"

"Hey, bro." Wes trotted downstairs and cut off her admission. Upon spotting the baby on Minka's lap, he hollered for Caela. "Honey, Tyson's here!"

Madness ensued, with the giddy little girl's footsteps bustling into the room. She always did her best to entertain her baby cousin with her old toys and funny faces. Wes sat beside his brother to chat, so Minka withdrew her theory from her lips. Considering the perfect timing, she had to wonder if her husband staged the distraction. Before long, his rascally wink confirmed her suspicions.

Relieved to a degree, she didn't call him out, but she continued to grapple over it. The conspiracy theories made hers and Renee's silence even riskier, given the entire department could be painted as conspirators if Everett's partner surfaced. Then again, she supposed, keeping them all in the dark could prove to be protection if that were the case.

Finally, Cael put her mind at rest, proving too good of a detective to let the matter drop. When the kids' volume lowered, he tapped Minka's shoulder. "What were you saying about the case?"

She averted her gaze from Wes, in an effort not to lose her nerve. "Well, as I contemplated everything the other night, I remembered how the bomber wanted the blueprints to the courthouse. If Everett acted alone, I can't figure out why he'd need them. His history should've given him all the means to plot it out, especially considering how he already managed to hide his theft when he worked there. I can only conclude he had an accomplice, who was probably the mastermind in the first place."

Cael's brow shot up. "That's a lot to absorb."

"Tell me about it," she replied.

He leaned forward and put his elbows on his knees. "Okay, let's talk this through. If Everett had a partner, the partner most likely selected him because of his knowledge. Even in that scenario, why put out an ad for the blueprints?"

"Like I told Renee, Everett could've been responding to the ad or he was a last-minute add-on after the bomber was eliciting them."

"You've run this by Renee?"

Minka nodded. "She didn't think we have enough to be certain of it, so she reckoned we're better off keeping mum about it and concentrate on locating Everett."

Cael didn't voice any judgement of the assessment, but from the way he scratched his chin, she discerned he didn't support it altogether. He grasped his phone again, scrolling back to the alleged photo of Everett. "This is probably just a regular surveillance snapshot of him making small talk with a stranger. We can't buy into a narrative that's framed by an unreliable, clearly biased source."

She murmured a word of agreement and sighed. "I wish I could say anyone could see through his act, but the people who want to smell smoke will."

He concurred with her, before Tyson started to fuss, this time over his cousin taking the stuffed horse out of his hands. Caela protested that she wanted to give him a chance to play with a tugboat, instead. Regardless, the kiddy spat broke up the speculating for the evening. Even so, Minka continued to ponder the ordeal and what headaches it would inflict on Gus.

She didn't give into her urge to text him about it, but his expression Tuesday morning made his frustration obvious. She decided not to touch the matter right away, allowing him some space. She didn't have to wait long, however, to hear his feelings.

He stepped out of his office moments after their shift began and addressed the room. "Listen up, guys. I'm sure everyone has heard or read about the photo of Everett by now. I, personally, think it's a bunch of hoopla, but Chief Friedman says otherwise. He's sending Internal Affairs out here to launch an investigation. I appreciate that it's a pain, but let's just cooperate so we can get back to work."

"Anyone can see that picture's a fraud," Cael said, evoking a murmur of agreement.

"Well, the chief's never been known for his vision."

The cheeky remark, out of character for the lieutenant, netted snickers and cheers throughout the precinct. Meanwhile, Minka shook her head over the toll this pressure was taking on her friend, as dark bags now lay under his eyes. She sat down in front of her computer and accessed the inflammatory article to read it over again. Her indignation provoked her to make a decision many would've avoided.

"We need to talk to Steward," she told Renee. "If he really has proof of this bombshell, he owes it to his city to present us with all the facts."

Chapter Six

After days of dreading having to face her partner every day, Minka stifled a chuckle when she spotted the same misery in Renee's eyes over having to speak to Finn Steward. A groan escaped Renee's throat just before they entered the building that served as the headquarters of his online media outlet. Granted, the prospect didn't thrill Minka, either, given her previous run-ins with the reporter. His office wasn't large enough to contain his ego and his respect for authority would fit in a pen cap. Unlike her partner, however, Minka had enjoyed a six-year respite from his insolent ways, making her ready to battle.

Two other reporters, a man and a woman, sat at their desks in the small room; they both leveled dastardly smiles at the detectives. They appeared to share Steward's contemptuous attitude which fogged the entire space even without his presence. Minka and Renee didn't have to ask to meet with him before the woman tapped on her boss's door.

Steward sauntered out wearing a smug grin below his patchy moustache. "Detectives, I suspected we'd be meeting soon. Nice to see you again, Detective Avery. You know, you truly are an inspiration. Not many people could just decide the city was safe enough to leave it behind to go off and raise a kid for six years. Thank goodness you emerged from domestication when you did."

"I trusted I was leaving things in your capable hands," she sneered. "After all, what's one less donut-lover on the force going to cost the city?"

Renee entered the match of wits. "Yes, we were on our way to the bakery and wanted to stop in to applaud yet another one of your gifts to journalism and society. Without you, I can't fathom how civil unrest would continue."

"I just report the truth, ladies."

Minka used his own words against him. "Then, as citizens of this city and two of your readers, we want to hear the truth of who your sources for this article are."

Steward didn't wince, pointing to the sign hanging beside his door, which boasted the first amendment. "You'll have to take that up with our founding fathers."

"This is an open investigation, and one that concerns national security. Withholding information warrants an arrest," Renee warned.

"Detectives, I appreciate you're doing your job, and you must understand I'm doing mine. If I give up my sources—to whom I swore confidentiality—I lose my reputation."

Renee crossed her arms. "You can either be a traitor to your sources or a traitor to your city, which you claim to love so much."

"If you don't cooperate, we will get a warrant to search your office and home," Minka added. "While we're at it, we may even refer you to the feds."

Steward put his hands in his pockets and abandoned his high and mighty platform for the moment. "The truth is, I don't actually know who they are. As the article stated, an unknown source emailed me the photo. I replied and requested an interview, but they would only answer my questions online. I can't even say if it was a man or a woman."

"Do you have your correspondence?" Minka asked.

He nodded and agreed to pass it on to them. Minka forwarded it to the department's tech guy on the way back to the station, in hopes he could uncover more than they could and at a faster pace.

When they returned to the precinct, Internal Affairs had already arrived and begun interviewing every officer one by one. Calling them back in alphabetical order, they were interviewing Cael, meaning Minka would be next. She had nothing to hide, but a disconcerting instinct lurked inside her. She tried her best to remain calm, but still, a shiver ran through her upon hearing her name.

Sergeant Maureen Wallace invited her to take a seat on the opposite side she was used to in the interrogation room and began the discussion. "Detective Avery, is my understanding correct that you're new to the department?"

"In a way. I was here for over four years, then I left for six after I had my daughter."

"I see," the sergeant replied, her eyes conveying the same opinion Renee and Finn Steward held about her extended maternity leave. "And you came back the week of the bombing?"

Sick about what the lady may be insinuating, Minka could only throw out an uncomfortable joke. "Talk about returning with a bang."

As Sergeant Wallace made a note of her remark, she regretted her words and started to attempt to clarify them. Before she could, Wallace's partner, Camden

Radcliffe, grilled her over her departure from the force and different aspects of her personal life. Eventually, they asked about the state of the investigation. She gave them a general synopsis, but they wanted details. She didn't have a problem with it, until Radcliffe questioned, "You arrested Everett's ex, Peta Lawson, only to drop the charges two days later. Why?"

"She cooperated with us and proved that she didn't have a hand in his exploits like we originally suspected."

Radcliffe raised his eyebrow. "What do you mean by that?"

"She complied with our request to call him, and she also divulged more details about their encounter before he went on the run."

Wallace didn't miss a beat. "She acknowledged they were in contact?"

Treading carefully because of how little they told the chief about the arrest, Minka admitted, "Only after we found proof. We noticed a box of hair dye in the trash, so we cornered her into confessing that Everett had used it."

Wallace kept her gaze on her notes. "How long did it take her to admit it belonged to him?"

"Until she realized she didn't have a choice," she replied, aware she was closing in on the boundary of deception. "Like I said, we didn't release her before we had the whole story."

To her surprise, the two IA hacks backed down, and the conversation ended after a couple of trivial inquiries. Minka let out a deep sigh of relief when she made it to her desk and collapsed into her chair.

Renee, who didn't seem to detect her agony,

looked preoccupied by another matter. "Jeremy just tracked the origin of the messages from Steward's informant to a café an hour away. Let's go."

****

While they doubted they'd catch Steward's source at the café, Minka and Renee hoped his or her visit would've been captured on surveillance footage. They called the place and verified the business had cameras and would be able to retrieve it from the period in question. Since the messages between the pair were time-stamped, they could locate the timeframe without trouble. The long drive proved to be their biggest hurdle.

For the entire journey to Mount Dora, Minka kept mulling over her meeting with Internal Affairs. She couldn't fully understand her own unwillingness to confide in the sergeants, as it was common to try to coerce a suspect back onto the grid by using loved ones. She also realized that her reluctance could get her into more trouble if they perceived it. Between the chief and Steward's article, along with the disparaging attitude they manifested about her family life, she supposed her guard instinctively snapped up.

With each passing mile, she continued to debate whether or not to discuss the matter with Renee, realizing that her tongue would be wagging at full speed if Cael sat beside her. As much as she wanted to get off the ledge and trust her partner, she simply couldn't do it yet. She'd done so when she revealed her theory of Everett having an accomplice, but that didn't free her inside. Instead, she ended up more constrained than before, violating her own ethics to show loyalty and faith in Renee. That in mind, she opted to keep mum for the time being and keep their conversation light.

Upon parking in front of the café, the detectives stepped out of Renee's car. The manager greeted them at the door, his electronic tablet in hand. They cued up the footage to the previous Sunday morning. At the very moment the informant would've been contacting Steward, there were just three customers. Shockingly, none of them were even using their phone.

"That's a rarity, not just for an internet café, but a line to a port-a-pot," Renee said.

They scanned through the video, in case the time stamp was off or showing a different time zone. While several did have their phones in hand at various times, they didn't employ them long enough to have typed the lengthy message sent to Steward.

"Maybe he had it ready to go and simply had to tap send," Minka reasoned aloud, thinking in terms of what she'd done in the past. She asked the manager, "How far out does your Wi-Fi signal reach?"

"Most of the front lot and about half of the back," he reported.

"Are those areas under surveillance?"

"Sure are." He tapped onto another vantage point.

Going back to the time of suspicion, they slowed it down when a green truck parked near the entrance, matching the description of one Everett owned. On her phone, Minka confirmed the license plates were a match. Her jaw dropped. "Everett is Steward's informant?"

"Jerk," Renee muttered. "This must be his retaliation against us for arresting Peta. He mocked up a photo to put the department back into the line of fire."

"Well done," Minka murmured.

The detectives took a copy of the footage on a thumb drive and headed back to the precinct. During the trip, Minka couldn't help but wonder what this meant. At first glance, it was a major breakthrough, which could give them all back their good name. On the other hand, the public—and even Internal Affairs—could believe Everett, given that he, more than anyone, would know with whom he was working. Without much persuasion, the so-called villain of the story could suddenly transform into the corruption-exposing vigilante.

Yet again, Minka worried over the possibility of their phony arrest being discovered. To truly convince people of Everett's bad motives, they'd have to mention it. With Internal Affairs already on their case, they would delve deeper into the matter and may well deem Minka's testimony deceptive.

Unable to suppress her anxieties anymore, she confronted them with Renee. "You don't figure this will appease Internal Affairs, do you?"

"In our dreams."

"Do you reckon they'll have a problem with Peta's arrest?"

"What about it? Aren't they up to speed on the details?"

Minka backed off, recalling that Gus had privately told her his wish to keep the particulars under wraps. "I guess."

"The boss would be an idiot to be secretive with the chief." Renee slid a sidelong glance over, appearing to be onto her partner. When Minka remained silent, she continued, "I wouldn't expect them to disapprove of it. It's one of the oldest tricks in the book. If I sense they don't like it, that's exactly what I'll tell them."

Her words sent shivers through Minka, who hadn't even factored that hitch into the equation. Renee was set to talk with Internal Affairs in a few hours, tops, and if their accounts conflicted, she could land in serious trouble. Then again, she wouldn't help her case by coaching her not to be truthful.

Without a clue of what else to do, Minka asked her to stop for a restroom break, with the intent to call Gus. Locking herself in, she frantically dialed and ground her teeth when he didn't answer. Starting to text him, her shaky hands almost fumbled the phone when it began to vibrate.

"Give me good news, Minks," Gus greeted her, his voice unusually gruff.

She'd wished he'd be the one with good news. "Well, we figured out who Steward's informant is."

"Thank you," he cried.

"Not so fast…it's Everett."

Gus caught onto the runaway's motive right away. "We take his woman, so he makes our lives miserable. So, where does that leave us?"

"I was hoping you could help me with that."

He paused to deliberate. "I mean, it doesn't truly clear us, even though it seems to be an act of revenge. After the last forty-five minutes I've spent with Internal Affairs, I'm afraid it's going to take a lot to get them off our backs."

She agreed, and despite hating to worsen the dilemma, she had no time to waste. "That's actually why I called. How much do they and the chief know about the ex's arrest?"

"More than ever now, after they grilled me on it. I never fully confessed that it was staged, but I have a feeling they surmised it."

"I revealed as little as I could. Do you think they'll accuse me of giving a false statement?"

"I wouldn't sweat it. If anyone has to pay for this, it'll be me."

The comment gave her no solace. "Renee has to sit down with them later, and she doesn't realize how much we've kept them in the dark. Should I say something to her?"

He paused. "No, that could make this even messier. She's good at what she does, but I don't know her well enough to put my full trust in her."

"How kind of you to trust her enough to partner us together."

He snorted. "I trusted you to be able to handle her."

****

Snuggling on the couch with her feverish little girl, Minka had never enjoyed having a sick child until that moment. The school called her not long after Renee's interview with Internal Affairs concluded, and her rigid partner didn't disclose anything about the exchange. Instead of calling Wes, his mom, or Lola, Minka picked Caela up, in need of a partial mental health day. She didn't deem monitoring her temperature and all too soon cleaning up vomit the best of stress-relievers, but she took solace in her safe haven.

Before receiving the call, she consulted with Jeremy about the photo, wondering if he could decipher whether or not it'd been manipulated. Though he didn't have the expertise, he had a friend who did and emailed it to her. Until they could deem it a fake, they resolved not to leak the fact that Everett was the mysterious informant.

With Wes in parent-teacher conferences, Minka cradled her helpless daughter while watching television. Since she could no longer stand up with the growing girl in her arms, she carried in her dinner before she sat down and was munching on it when her phone vibrated. She expected it to be Wes informing her he was on his way, but Lola's photo illuminated the screen.

After exchanging greetings, Lola asked, "How's Caela doing? Ryan said she wasn't feeling well at lunch, and then, Gus told us you had to leave work early."

"She's seen better days, and I won't go into what I've seen. Let's just say I'm eating dinner late because I didn't have an appetite an hour ago."

The fellow mom giggled. "Sounds like the flu they've been warning about on the news. I can take her tomorrow, if you need."

"Thank you, but Jaclyn's going to. You don't need this. How are you feeling, by the way?"

"Pretty great. I still have my nauseous moments, but my appetite's in full swing. My husband seems to be the one with the crazy hormones."

Tickled by her friend's analysis of Gus's demeanor, Minka laughed and tried to keep the conversation light. "I had the same trouble with Wes."

"I'm serious, Minka. One minute, he's the life of the party, dying his hair and riding around in a sports car, and the next, he's all grouchy and in bed before Ryan goes down."

"Lola, Wes hunted for another job across the country, meddled in my case, and was almost killed by the mob—all in my first trimester! I swear, he could smell that I was pregnant, and it made him restless."

"You think it's the baby, then?"

Minka didn't want her friend to develop a complex about herself and her unborn child, so she set her joking aside. "He's really excited about the little one, trust me. Guys just get weird when they encounter changes in general."

"I guess you're right. A new baby, a new house: it's a lot, even for me. Did he tell you we have a buyer?"

Minka gulped due to the instability at work, but she did her best to disguise her reservations. "No, he didn't. Congratulations. Is the deal done?"

"Not yet. They're in the process of applying for financing. They offered less than our asking price, but our agent had us aim high in the first place. Besides, it's a young couple, who has a baby due the week before ours, so we both have the same idea. Gus still won't put an offer on the one we want until their loan's approved. I just don't understand him sometimes."

"Join the club," Minka told her, wondering when he'd come to his senses and be upfront with his wife.

Lola laughed about her dry remark, her spirits clearly lifted as the conversation wound down. Minka continued to contemplate the couple long after she hung up, empathetic to the position in which both of them found themselves. She may not have agreed with Gus's secrecy, but in the end, she understood it. She remembered her own agony when, in her fourth month of pregnancy, Wes emerged from WITSEC without a clue of whether or not he'd be reinstated to his job. When the school welcomed him back with open arms, their worry seemed to be a needless threat to unborn Caela. Gus, no doubt, hoped to spare his family the same anxiety.

Even so, Minka could only envision this not ending well. She wanted to keep faith in her innocent commanding officer, but the odds were stacked against him. While Internal Affairs couldn't accuse Gus of wrongdoing, they could raise their ethics to a level higher than he could measure up to. If they wanted to take issue with Peta's arrest or even the information they'd withheld about Everett that day, they had the means and platform to act on it.

Just before her worst-case-scenarios spiraled out of control, she received a group text from Jeremy to her, Renee, and Gus.

—*Definitely a phony.*—

—*Yes!*—she replied.

The guys exchanged a back and forth about the details. Not only did Jeremy's friend deem the photo a fake, she had a colleague verify it, as well, and both agreed to attest to it in public. With the facts settled, Gus alerted Chief Friedman, who informed the press of their discovery.

The media release reaped the expected results, with half of the public believing them, while the other half gave way to more conspiracy theories. Minka took it in stride, too concerned about carting Caela over to her in-laws' Wednesday morning. Not to her surprise, cameras and reporters greeted her at the precinct, after which she listened to the sixteen voicemails awaiting her response on her work phone from various outlets. Everyone vied for a comment about this theory or that, which she denied.

Renee, Gus, Cael, and Declan faced the same frenzy. Of all the calls they received, however, one reporter in particular stayed mum, rousing suspicion.

"Have any of you heard from Steward?" Gus asked the four detectives before their lunch break.

When they confirmed they hadn't, Cael said, "Guess we took the wind out of his sails."

"I'm afraid he has self-inflating ones," Minka replied. "He's not one to be shamed. With all of the conspiracies out there, he's probably ready to take hold of one and drop another bomb—no pun intended."

Gus sighed. "I suppose."

When the other three resumed their work, Minka rose from her desk and caught him before he retreated to his office. "Don't you think you ought to clue Lola in on some of this?"

"I have. I just didn't disclose the parts that involve me."

"Everything involves you."

"That's why it was such a brief conversation."

Minka didn't have a chance to reply before Sergeant Wallace wandered over, stone-faced.

"Lieutenant, may we have a word?"

****

To Minka's relief, Gus's interview with the sergeants ended twenty minutes later, and he carried on with his work. She restrained her urge to follow him into his office, wanting to give him space as well as to remain professional. Even so, she kept a watchful eye on him, in attempts to read his expression and to ensure he wasn't packing up his belongings.

Riddled with unspoken curiosity, she couldn't keep bottling it up and decided to direct some of it Renee's way. "Did they grill you about Peta's arrest?"

"Not really. When they mentioned it, I just said we did what we had to do."

"And you didn't go into details about it being staged?"

"No, I didn't feel like I needed to. They seemed to already be aware."

The exchange only roused her inquisitiveness, so she backed down. Unable to focus on anything else, she gave up and grabbed her phone to text Gus. After all, no one would notice, and if he needed his privacy, he could merely ignore the message.

—*How'd it go?*—

Through his window, she observed him grab his phone, then glance up at her.

—*I'm still here, aren't I?*—

—*Renee said they're filled in about Peta?*—

—*Will you get over Peta?*—

She shot him a scowl, which he reciprocated with a smirk of satisfaction, and she not-so-subtly dropped her phone. Albeit frustrated, she found solace in the fact that it didn't seem to concern him much, meaning the issue didn't put his job at risk. If they didn't have anything against him, however, why else would they ask to talk with him a second time?

Liable to go crazy pondering it, she forced her mind to focus on work. She checked Everett's financials and phone records, but neither divulged anything new. With the screen showing the same results every day, she became more and more disheartened, figuring he wouldn't slip up as time passed. He probably destroyed the phone and credit cards on file by now and had taken on another identity. Until they discovered what—or, rather, who—that was, they could only hope someone would recognize him and have the guts to report it.

Everett's pride, too, could play to their advantage. He stayed in the general area and framed the police department, when he could've fled the country long before then. He may not have been rich, but eight-hundred bucks—plus whatever he had in cash—would have been enough to get him to Mexico, if not Canada, according to his wish. Sticking in the state, though, only increased his chances of being caught. She continued to wonder what perks his supposed getaway plan involved and assumed he still hadn't secured it.

Minka wasn't a profiler, but experience with criminals taught her that they enjoyed the risk, and more than that, they reveled in the ensuing chaos they caused. As in most terrorist attacks, he'd wanted to prove a point and no doubt ate up the countless times the news replayed their coverage. Plus, he added to his celebrity by posting the photo and getting Steward's attention. Rather than fleeing to preserve his life, he'd take his chances while basking in his own notoriety.

Sickened by the thought, Minka snapped out of her trance when her work phone rang, but Steward's voice took her right back. "Detective, I wanted to inform you Mr. Everett contacted me and wants to meet up."

The fact that he'd give them a heads-up sent her head spinning, but she decided not to question it. Nonetheless, she wondered about Everett's logic when Steward related how he chose The Froggy Wetlands as their rendezvous point. A popular tourist attraction, the place wouldn't give them any privacy.

She and Renee scrambled to get there, rounding up

the SWAT team for good measure. As they drove, Renee voiced questions similar to Minka's. "Why in the world would Everett return to town? Better yet, why would he want to meet Steward on an airboat?"

Minka pictured the setting. "For the same reason he took a bunch of souvenirs for his getaway wardrobe— to blend in with the tourists. While people may be aware of him, they wouldn't necessarily notice him in their vacation bliss. Even the workers might not recognize him since it's such an unlikely hangout for a terrorist."

"Airboats are so noisy, though. How could they even have a conversation? Cliff and I took the grandkids last year; I couldn't hear myself talk."

"Who says they have to talk?" Minka asked, being an expert on inaudible communication. "Maybe they'll just pass notes back and forth or something."

"What is this? Fourth grade? In this day and age, why would a wanted felon lure the city's biggest gossiper out here, just to hand him notes? He could easily send him messages from the safety of his hide-out."

"But those can be tracked. That's how we outed him as Steward's source yesterday," Minka replied. "There's no way Everett would anticipate Steward looping us in on this."

When they arrived at the dock, they found Steward, leaning against his car, waiting. He held a paper in his hand, which Minka assumed was for his own notes. They started to go ahead with their plan of parking a distance away from him, but he waved them over. After commanding the SWAT unit to stand down, Renee drove to where the reporter stood.

"He's gone," Steward told them after the women got out of their vehicle.

"What do you mean he's gone?" Renee cried.

"I was walking up to the boat, like he instructed, and someone bumped into me. When I spun around to give him a piece of my mind, I spotted this note on the ground. By the time I read his signature, he vanished."

"How long does it take you to read?" Renee asked.

"Not as long as it would take for me to catch him," the middle-aged, tubby man admitted.

Minka asked him for the note and read it aloud. "*For your sake and mine, Mr. Steward, I deem it best we limit our time face-to-face. I apologize if the unauthenticity of my photo called your credibility into question, but rest assured, despite its being a facsimile, what it represents is true. There is a dirty cop in Orlando, who had a greater role in this than I, and who promised me the immunity I'm obviously not receiving. I will not reveal his identity since I consider it's the OPD's duty to unmask the mole amongst them. I'm warning them, however, that continuing to pursue me could lead them to more than they've bargained for.*"

Renee shook her head. "So, he's basically saying, 'I lied, but I'm actually telling the truth.' Yeah, that makes a lot of sense. He's just messing with us. He was caught, and his big showstopper was about to disappear, so he has to make another headline."

Steward plucked the note out of Minka's hand. "And indeed, he will."

"You can't print this," Minka said.

Steward's usual smug grin reappeared. "Says who? I merely agreed to have you guys tag along, which was a favor, if I may add. I never claimed any of this was off the record. In fact, your actions were always going to be a part of the storyline."

Renee glared. "Well, in that case, how are we to believe this isn't all a ruse? Who's to say you didn't lure us out here, just for a good, juicy story? Maybe you wrote that note."

"Perjury's a serious crime," Minka added.

"You're right, Detectives; I did come here for an exclusive, but it wasn't about petty little policewomen. Yesterday was the worst day of my career, and I consider myself fortunate to still have a job. I need redemption, and more than that, I wanted answers from a dirtbag who nearly cost me everything."

Minka made a final attempt to salvage the venture of calling out SWAT on a whim. It would be enough to send the chief over the moon—and add fuel to his current rant against his officers. "How did he get ahold of you?"

"By phone. I kept the number."

Renee rolled her eyes. "How nice of you to be so forthcoming."

Right after Minka dialed the number, a nearby phone began to ring. Scanning the area, she spotted it laying on the ground. She bent down to pick it up but recoiled when she saw the numbers on the screen counting down.

"Everybody run!" she screamed.

The crowd dashed toward the other side of the parking lot.

An instant later, an empty boat exploded.

Chapter Seven

When Minka entered the house, she found Wes and Caela on the couch, watching the news on the television. She cringed over Wes allowing their daughter to listen to the disturbing reports about the Froggy Wetlands Bombing, but she couldn't rebuke him. Caela may well learn about it at school, so they'd be better off confronting it as a family. Drawn in by the coverage of the chaos on the screen, she didn't make a peep—at first.

The anchor faced the camera, with the remains of the explosion behind her. "Froggy Wetlands transformed into more than a popular tourist attraction today. Just after noon, a currently unused airboat exploded, setting the boat and its surroundings on fire. Officials say they recovered remnants of a bomb much like the one used in the courthouse bombing last week. The fire has been contained, but the adjacent boathouse suffered substantial damage. Thankfully, there were only a few minor injuries, due in part to Detective Minka Avery of the Orlando Police Department.

"Detective Avery and her partner, Detective Renee Hart, were, in another surprising twist, working with reporter Finn Steward. After the prime suspect in the courthouse bombing, Silas Everett, contacted him, Steward alerted the detectives. It is believed Everett wanted to have his say after authorities exposed the photo he leaked to the press of himself with an alleged dirty cop to be a fraud. According to Steward, however, Everett merely handed him a note, which he'll make public tomorrow. Shortly thereafter, Detectives Avery and Hart arrived and after calling Everett's phone, discovered it to be acting as a detonator, which had begun to count down. That was when Avery yelled for everyone to run, saving the lives of nearly thirty awaiting passengers."

Minka groaned when her image appeared on the screen with soot all over her face. Their choice to use closed captions to translate her speech didn't boost her confidence, either, but she understood. "I'm relieved no one was badly hurt, but this is far from a win in any of our books. This goes to show how dangerous and crafty Silas Everett is, and we're working all angles to stop him. To our utter frustration, though, we've been unsuccessful so far and appreciate any information that may be out there."

In real time, she stepped into the living room and set down her bag on the end table. "The reporter's makeup team was there, but they wouldn't do anything for me."

As one, Wes and Caela pivoted, then her distressed little girl ran into her arms. Wes lagged behind a bit, but Minka noticed him wipe away the stray tear from his eye. As he embraced them both, she hoped her family couldn't sense her quivering. Despite the hours that had passed since the explosion, her nerves remained tense. During the tender moment, she closed her eyes and endeavored to focus on their love alone.

She and Wes sat as close together as possible on the couch, and she held Caela on her lap. The little one didn't seem to understand how to handle it all, but to Minka's surprise, she didn't ask any questions about her mother's experience. A few minutes later, she climbed down and retreated to her room for a while, until she returned with her piggy bank.

"Mommy, you can take my money and quit your job. It isn't a lot, but I think it's enough for some groceries."

"Thank you, baby, but that's your money for our next visit to Grammy and Pappy's house."

Her daughter's brown eyes welled up with tears. "But if you die at work, we might not even go."

The words broke her mother's heart in so many ways, and she could barely form a reply. She couldn't rightly tell her it wouldn't happen, but she had to reassure her child. "First of all, your grammy and pappy will always want you to visit them, whether I'm around or not. In fact, they'd need you more than ever. Today was scary for all of us, but I'm not a detective for the money, sweetie. I want to help people, and although this afternoon scared me, I'm happy I managed to do that. There were other mommies and daddies on that dock, who could've died if nobody had told them to run."

Caela nodded, seeming to absorb the matter as best as she could at her age, before she sought answers to another puzzle. "Why do people like to set off bombs?"

"Usually because they're angry," Minka stated.

"At what?"

"I don't know. Sometimes, I don't even think they do." Minka lifted her back onto her lap and kissed her forehead. "Like I said, my job is to keep people safe, and that includes you. Part of keeping you safe is keeping me safe, so I will always do everything I can to do that. Every time I leave this house for work, returning to you and Daddy is my biggest goal."

Caela smiled and accepted her mother's vow, snuggling into her. After that, the house fell quiet for most of the evening, all three of them recovering from the harrowing day. Caela retreated to bed an hour earlier than normal, but she wouldn't go to sleep unless Minka read her a bedtime story. She hadn't requested one in quite a while, so Minka discerned the day made her appreciate the fragileness of life and the simple pleasures with her mom.

The whole time, their painful conversation haunted Minka. She'd put up a strong front, but inside, her child's plea for her to quit the force stung deeply. The sentiment reawakened her doubts about why she'd returned to such a dangerous career. As she observed Caela drift into her slumber, she couldn't stop the tears from falling.

Waiting to leave the room until her daughter fell sound asleep, Minka trekked downstairs to rejoin Wes on the couch and laid her head on his shoulder. "What if she's right?" she asked him.

"Who?"

"Caela, about me quitting. I mean, what was I thinking, going back to this mayhem? You would've assumed I'd learned my lesson when it landed my husband in witness protection. Why was I yearning for this evil side of the world, when I should've been savoring every moment with that beautiful baby girl of ours?"

Wes caressed her shoulder. "Honey, don't go there again. This is what you love, and if you had only been a bystander to all of this, it would've driven you insane. I observed that for six years. There may have been a day when I despised the danger of your job, but after seeing how much you missed it, I wouldn't dare to coax you away from it again. And for the record, your career didn't land your husband in WITSEC; he did that all on his own!"

She snorted. "And it only took him six years to admit it."

Wes kissed her before padding into the kitchen for a snack. Her nerves finally relaxed a bit, until a forceful knock banged on the door. With caution, she stood and strode over to it.

Before she opened the door even halfway, her bounty hunter brother barreled inside and threw his sister over his shoulder. "It's my turn to protect you!"

"What on Earth are you doing? Let me down."

"No. You've always tried to keep me out of trouble, and now, it's time to repay the favor."

"And this is your way of doing that?"

Emerging from the kitchen, Wes all-too-casually greeted his brother-in-law, "Hey, man. Good to see you."

"You forgot to add, 'Put down my wife!' " Minka scolded.

"Nah, it's fine. He's known you longer than I have. I trust his judgement."

Minka didn't bother to make a knock on her husband's judgement over showing such trust in Robin. Instead, she continued to squirm until her brother conceded to her wishes, but he persisted in his argument. "You need to get out of here. Your precinct's corrupt, and you're being targeted by a terrorist."

"Says who?"

"The Internet."

She chose to ignore his poor choice in sources. "I appreciate your concern, but I'm fine. If a bomb doesn't kill me, nothing but frustration will."

"What exactly happened today?" he asked.

"Finn Steward lured us over there because Everett asked him to meet him there. By the time we arrived, Everett had already handed this note off and fled. It basically claimed that there is a rat in our precinct, and he just decided to use dishonest means to prove it. He even said we were in for it if we keep pursuing him."

Robin wouldn't give it up. "What'd I tell you?"

"It does sound like a threat, honey," Wes told her.

"It is, and if today tells us anything, it's that he isn't afraid to make good on his threats. We can only wish this was all he had in mind," she told them but immediately regretted her honesty when the determination on her brother's face intensified. "But I'm still not running away."

"Did surveillance capture him planting the bomb?" Wes asked.

She shook her head. "He chose a boat that was a distance from the building so there were no monitors around."

"Do you believe there's really a traitor among you?" Robin questioned.

"How can I say after ten days? I've hardly spoken to half of my colleagues. I don't want to buy into it, but this isn't a criminal's typical line of defense."

"Everett's not a typical criminal," Wes replied.

She acknowledged his point with a nod and glanced back at her brother. Aside from video games and technology, she'd never been inclined to ask for his advice. As the older and more successful sister, she took pride in being in the position to offer counsel, not receive it. In truth, she cringed to give him that leg up on her even once, but she couldn't ignore the resource he could be under these circumstances. "Any pointers on how to find someone?"

Despite her casual tone, Robin's chest expanded, making it clear that he detected the role reversal. "Well, my buddies and I often discuss where you guys go wrong in your tracking methods. I probably shouldn't give away our secrets in the interest of job security, but considering what's at stake, I'll let you in on one."

Minka bit her tongue and forced her eyes not to roll, while her brain—in her mother's voice—reminded her of his need for self-esteem.

He continued, "Remember why I hid out in your garage when I was on the run from the cops?"

"So you could sneak into our kitchen and swipe free snacks," she replied.

He snickered. "No, that was just a sweet byproduct. My main reason was the unlikelihood of it. You and I weren't on good terms, and you wouldn't have knowingly harbored me. Meanwhile, your detective friends and you were convinced Mom and Dad had me stashed away somewhere or that I must be at some other convenient place. Nobody would've suspected me right outside your door."

Minka smirked. "I can attest to that. I had to change my underpants after I caught you hunched behind the garbage bin."

"Too much info, sis. My point is, don't underestimate the craftiness of a runaway. I wasn't even guilty of a crime, but I schemed pretty well. Like Wes said, this Everett dude has skills. Stop trying to figure out where he'd flee under so-called normal circumstances."

"But how can we predict the unpredictable?" she asked in sincerity.

"You can't. What matters most of the time isn't what you deem a likely hideaway but what you completely rule out. Last year, a fugitive kidnapped his daughter, and I captured him while he was shopping with her at a toy store. An Amber Alert was out and everything, but no one expected him to have the guts to go into such a public place. Two policemen were even parked in the shopping plaza and didn't spot him."

As much as she didn't like to admit the flaws in the system, Minka bubbled with pride. Her brother, who'd been abducted when he was four by a devilish neighbor, now had a hand in saving children, too. Though he chose to do it in a different way than she did, she admired his courage to face such a scenario, especially given the emotional scars he still bore. "You're pretty awesome. Thanks for clueing me in on this. I'm sure you have your eyes peeled for Everett, too."

He smiled as she patted his arm, before he shrugged and put a damper on the bonding moment with his typical line of reasoning. "I'm not going to expend a great deal of effort until you and the feds up your reward. My guys and I can't believe you've put a measly five grand on a terrorist's head. Do you think they'll raise it now that you were almost killed?"

She blinked in response, unsure of what to say. Her sisterly ire returned, as she surmised the subject of money was his real motive for dropping by. "I take it you haven't caught your rocket man and cashed in his bounty."

"Nope. I didn't think as far outside the box as I should've in his case. Rumor has it he welcomed his kid into the world inside an RV at a rest stop. My buddies trekked off to Houston, betting on him to go to the launch pad there, but I'm not convinced. Besides, I'll be in pole position to snag Everett if you ever make it worth my while."

To her gratitude, the ring of her phone interrupted the bizarre conversation. When she read Gus's name, instantaneous unease settled into her stomach.

"I just wanted to make sure you're doing okay," he said.

She wanted to believe the claim, but his voice indicated more lay behind the call. She ignored her instincts for now. "Yeah, I was pretty rattled, but I'm happy to be home now."

"I'll bet you are." A long pause followed, during which Minka could almost hear him debating if he should continue. At last, he lowered the gauntlet. "I have an update. Freidman contacted me today. He said if we don't bring Everett in by Friday, he's going to replace me."

"That's ridiculous. You can't put a time-limit on a matter like this."

"Well, he technically hasn't. He's just put one on me."

Conviction surged through Minka. "Then, I guess we have two days to solve this."

****

Counting the brush strokes on the ceiling above her, Minka wondered why human nature made it hardest to sleep on the nights one needed it the most. While her determination to catch Everett ran stronger than ever, her confidence in actually doing so by the end of the week didn't burst at the seams. She spent her sleepless hours hashing and rehashing the case in its many frustrating complexities. All in all, she concluded they'd covered every lead to its potential, except for one—Everett's possible partner.

The theory gnawed at her still, and she wished she could've pursued it to greater lengths. True, just days had passed since the notion occurred to her, but she feared every moment they spent hunting down Everett alone gave his accomplice a chance to flee or devise another attack. He could've even planted the bomb at Froggy Wetlands, while Everett relaxed by a pool somewhere.

She pondered going public with her assumption, now that her initial reservations didn't hold much sway. The media already had the OPD pegged as the villains, and the chief was ready to boot out Gus. She feared making matters even worse, but she deemed it their only hope.

At the same time, she worried going against Renee's advice would constitute an act of betrayal. Though she was difficult to get along with, Minka respected her as both her partner and an older officer. She hadn't agreed with her plan to keep mum about her concern, but she wanted to maintain at least somewhat of a unified front.

By morning, she decided to give her a call and try to get her blessing of approval—or indifference, if nothing else. Renee didn't answer, however, so Minka left a message, casually stating that she wanted to run something by her. Caela rose soon after she hung up, still complaining of a bellyache. From the return of her skin color, her mother deduced she was better, but with her temperature still on the high side, both parents decided to let her miss one more day of school. Thus, Minka rushed to get her over to Jaclyn's, distracting her from her woes at work.

The minute she drove up to the precinct, they returned, especially when she had to navigate through the expanding crowd of press around the parking lot's entrance. With Renee's car yet to arrive, she glanced at her phone and confirmed that she hadn't called or texted her back. The development frustrated her, but in the end, it helped make her decision. After plopping her belongings onto her desk, she made a beeline to Gus's office.

She focused on maintaining a confident posture, attempting to conceal her nerves, much like she did during her investigation into Claire Pennbrook…

After her conversation with Justin Harris, Minka spent most of her night perusing Claire's exposés. In the few the paper had published, Claire showcased her talent for persuasive journalism and digging up juicy dirt. Her effectiveness made it more difficult to conclude who'd have it out for her. The politician she called out for mishandling campaign contributions had to withdraw his bid for mayor, and the farm she accused of inhumane practices ended up closing. Obviously, both subjects could foster ill will toward her.

As the evening progressed, Minka's optimism waned. Even with a mind full of well-founded suspicions, she didn't have many means to launch a thorough probe. The department wouldn't stand behind her if a suspect reported her for harassment. Besides, she questioned her own techniques, given how little time her training officer invested in her. Whatever possessed her to offer to assist Detective Channing?

The next day, she remembered her reason when she scanned through the missing persons reports and didn't find one on Claire. Frustrated, she wondered if Detwiler didn't give Detective Channing's report proper attention because of his low opinion of her. The notion strengthened her resolve to help Claire, but she struggled to determine the way to do so.

When Detective Channing's caller ID flashed on her phone, remorse pierced her. She didn't conceal her discouragement when she answered. "I have nothing to report, Detective. I'm afraid I have limited resources."

"Don't despair, Officer Parker. Even with the ones at my disposal, we still meet with dead ends."

She hated to inform him that his call to Detwiler didn't yield anything, but she figured he deserved a hint, at least. "I have yet to learn which detectives are assigned to the case. When I do, I'll pass on her phone and tell them everything I know."

She sensed that he read between the lines. "Have you scanned through it, by chance?"

"No, I'm uncomfortable invading her privacy."

"In our line of work, you have to get past boundary issues."

Flattered that he put them on the same level, she retrieved Claire's phone from her desk drawer. While he stayed on the line, she accessed the latest calls prior to all the ones Claire missed, and she discovered many originated from numbers Claire didn't have in her contacts. She told him she'd research them one-by-one, but for the moment, she accessed the calendar app. On the last day Claire showed any activity, she scheduled an interview with an unnamed source. When she tapped on it, an address and meeting time appeared.

"I have something interesting here, but I'll need a minute." Invigorated, her fingers whizzed across the keyboard to determine the location. She sighed when the result popped up. "According to my findings, she had a meeting with a mystery source in a vacant lot."

"Are you sure it's completely empty? Peer around the surroundings."

She followed his advice and spotted a structure in the back of the area. "I see maybe a shed or lean-to off the road a ways. Why would you arrange a meeting there?"

"Claire might not have known what awaited her. Could you grab another officer and check it out?"

She peeked around to learn if anyone was keeping tabs on her, but like always, none of her colleagues seemed clued in on her very existence. Still, she assured him, "Sure. We'll head right out."

The same unease brewed inside Minka as she entered Gus's office to confess her theory of Everett's having an accomplice. She ordered herself not to deceive him this time, despite how troubling the truth was. Nonetheless, the scene tested her resolve. Clearly downhearted, her commanding officer had begun to strip the walls of his personal décor. The box on his desk held several framed photos of his family, along with his diploma from the academy and certificate for passing the lieutenants' exam. She observed him in silence for a brief moment, having never witnessed him so gloomy.

"Redecorating your office, Captain?"

"You might as well call me Civilian."

"We have more than twenty-four hours to snag the jerk, if not Everett."

He leveled a puzzled frown at her. "Isn't Everett the jerk?"

"No, Chief Friedman is."

He smirked. "Watch it, or I might have to reprimand you for disrespecting a commanding officer."

"As long as you're my CO, I don't mind. That said, the friend in me hopes you fessed up to your wife."

"I'd be a fool not to."

"How'd she take it?"

"I wouldn't know. She hasn't said a word since I sprung it on her. Call me crazy, but I thought the words, 'Honey, I'm probably going to lose my job in two days,' would surely be a conversation starter, even if it wasn't a pleasant one."

Minka pursed her lips and lowered her head. Although she didn't want to appear to be prying, she couldn't repress her curiosity. "What's going on with your housing situation?"

"Our deal is done, and we close in two weeks. The buyer negotiated with our realtor to have us out within ten days after that, so I'm guessing we'll have to rent a place. The timing stinks, but I guess it's for the best. We'll get out of a mortgage until I figure out what I'm going to do with my life—at forty-two years old, with a wife and two kids."

Her heart broke for them all, and she kept silent for a minute. She forced the words out before her nerves could overtake her. "In keeping with making confessions, I have something to get off my chest, too."

Gus listened to her reasoning about Everett not needing the blueprints and her thoughts of another party being involved. "So, you're telling me there could be a terrorist on the loose, who thinks he's free, unless Everett squeals?"

"Possibly. I realize I should've told you sooner, but with the press and Freidman, then the photo surfaced, and—"

"Hold up—the photo," he interrupted her, grabbing the picture. "Suppose this is his partner."

"Both Jeremy and his associate say it's a fake."

"No, if I'm not mistaken, it's the supposed badge that was doctored. We'll have to verify it, but I believe the other person is the real deal. Everett could've responded to the ad for information on the courthouse, and this might've been their strategizing session."

"Do you really think they'd deliberate in public, where anybody could eavesdrop, instead of plotting online?"

"Whoever claimed online exchanges are secure? Lola just emailed her aunt about the baby, and now, she's being barraged with ads for diaper rash ointment."

Studying the photo again, Minka sighed. "There's so little to go off of here. You can barely make out the face, and from the stance, I can't even tell if it's a guy or a woman."

"Which is why we shouldn't focus on the person but the surroundings," Gus said.

Despite having her reservations about his logic, she humored him and soon noted a familiar blue edge just beyond their heads. She pointed to it. "That's a table canopy behind them. They were standing outside the diner across from the courthouse."

****

As she drove to the diner, Renee dished out the silent treatment again, so the air hung thick with tension in the car. She didn't approve of her partner defying her recommendation and wanted to make that clear. Minka told her she called to debate it with her, but Renee insisted that she would've waited if she really cared. Minka couldn't argue, aware she'd made up her mind before she even called. Unable to reveal the dire straits Gus was in, however, she couldn't explain her reasons for the sudden change of heart.

The diner had recovered well in the short time that passed since the explosion, showing few signs of the destruction it witnessed. The debris-covered tables appeared almost new with bright blue table canopies hanging over them; only the broken picture window remained unrepaired. Renee pointed out the security camera attached to the building, which probably snapped the incriminating photo. Minka strategized how Everett might've obtained it.

In spite of it being so busy, Dawson spotted them right away and offered a friendly wave while he finished his chat with an apparent regular.

"It's good to see you guys again. You here for a well-deserved pancake breakfast?"

The comment heightened the enticing aroma of bacon and pastries that saturated the air. "I wish, believe me," Minka replied. "I assume you've been following the news?"

"I don't even have to try around here," Dawson told them, motioning toward the room full of newspaper-reading customers. By now, many lowered their copies to stare at the renowned detectives.

Renee tapped on her phone, displaying the photo of Everett and his possible partner. "I'm sure this had the tongues wagging."

"You're not kidding."

Minka zoomed in on the image. "We wondered if you recognized either of them? It looks like they were standing outside your diner."

He scrutinized it. "They do appear to be right outside, but no, I'm sorry. Neither strikes me as familiar. I've been studying Everett's face on the news, wishing I could give you something, but I've honestly never seen him."

"It's okay. We appreciate your eagerness and time," Minka told him. "If this was captured by your surveillance camera, Everett must have hacked into your system. Did you get any alerts about your software being compromised?"

He shook his head. "If anything came through, I missed it. Granted, my security system isn't as strong as you'd expect of an ex-law enforcer. Trust me, that'll change soon." Before Renee took the photo from him, he zoomed in even more. "Look closer at the back of that cap. It's hard to tell, but that's the logo for the Young Masters Martial Arts Division. My oldest son goes to the center for his karate classes."

Eyeballing it harder, Minka just barely made out the colorful circle decal, but she had faith in his deduction. "You may have left the force, Michaels, but you're still a natural."

Her compliment made him smile, after which he and the detectives exchanged farewells. On their silent drive back to the precinct, Minka couldn't help but wish she could've switched him out with Renee. Even so, she trudged along in her day, her first matter of business being to enlist Jeremy's expertise in blowing up the picture to better examine the logo on the mystery man's cap. The image blurred a little, but it matched the insignia they found online, a silhouette of two people bowing to each other in front of a bonsai tree.

She and Renee made the thirty-minute trek to the studio, only a few sentences spoken between them. When they arrived and didn't discover anyone but the cleaning crew, both vented their mutual frustration. It was a wasted trip, and glancing over at the clock on the dash, all Minka could focus on was Gus's livelihood running out of time.

Nonetheless, they didn't give up on their efforts. Once back at their desks, they combed through the center's social media pages, in an attempt to catch sight of anyone resembling Everett's companion. It proved to be a more daunting task than anticipated, with so many videos posted of the programs' many practices and competitions. Of course, the wrestler in Cael had to join his sister-in-law after taking a glance at her screen.

"Man, why don't I ever get assignments like this?" Cael joked.

"Speak for yourself. This is as tedious to me as binge-watching romantic movies would be to you."

"Enough said, but if my wife asks, those chick flick marathons are much better than watching sports on Saturday afternoons," he replied. "But back to this, what's going on? Is Everett into karate or something?"

"I don't know but it appears his friend in the photo he posted was active in it. Dawson spotted this studio's logo on his cap."

"You're getting tips from Dawson again? Wes is going to be jealous, given the fit you throw when he gets involved in a case." He jabbed her shoulder in jest. "Wasn't the picture a fraud, anyways?"

She passed on Gus's logic from that morning, then nodded at the photo. "So, we're hoping this guy leads us closer to Everett or some element of the case. I've viewed over twenty videos, though, and haven't caught a glimpse of anyone who remotely resembles him."

Cael patted her back and stayed to observe the rest of the match between the teenage students. "That kid's at least a year younger than his opponent, but he's beating the crap out of him."

"Bring back memories?" she teased, dodging another playful punch. The exchange boosting her morale, the clouds of her weariness no longer impeded her vision. "Wait a minute—is that him?"

She paused the frame that captured the student's apparent father, and Cael released a doubtful murmur. "Maybe. It's hard to tell since we can't zero in on his face in the photo. Sure, same hat and build, but those two things are fairly common among these types of dads."

Getting a better angle on him a few frames later, Minka stopped it again. "It's him. The height, the jawline—they're spot-on. Now, we just have to figure out his kid's name."

"Well, the comments say that Chandler Turner beats Alex O'Malley, so we just have to see who wins."

"Great. Let's skip to the end," she said, starting to toggle over to the final seconds of the timeline.

"Hey, now—" He swatted her hand off the mouse.

"—there's only a minute left. Savor the suspense."

Rolling her eyes, she gave in without dispute. She'd never admit it, but as the match peaked to its climax, her adrenaline kicked into high gear. She didn't understand the logistics of it too well, until the older kid fell to the ground, and the referee lifted up the younger's hand.

"We have a winner; Chandler Turner's dad is our mystery man," Minka announced.

****

Despite Minka and Cael's breakthrough, they couldn't do much without the karate studio's help. She searched through public records, but with two other young men sharing the name, she couldn't deduce which matched the kid in the video. Minka called Dawson to determine if he was acquainted with them, but since his son was younger than Chandler, the families never met. Thus, everything remained in a waiting pattern until the studio reopened.

Minka's excitement over possibly identifying Everett's partner vanished as soon as she observed a hopeless Gus exit the precinct that evening. The clock's ticking grew louder, and optimism and possibilities wouldn't silence it. They had to find solid answers by tomorrow, or he would be forced to march out of his office for good.

Mulling over the dire situation, her musings switched to poor Lola. She wondered if Gus admitted that she'd been in on his secret, and she worried over how it would impact their friendship. They just had the conversation about his changing attitude two nights prior, and Minka encouraged her to sluff off her concerns. With his alarming news the very next day,

Lola likely added everything up and may well have viewed her friend's misleading advice as an act of betrayal.

Unable to handle the consuming uncertainty, she used the hands-free feature on her SUV to call Lola while driving home. Since Gus had a longer journey than she did, she hoped to catch her before he arrived and maybe get her into a better humor for his homecoming. The instant she heard her voice, though, she doubted her ability to cheer her.

"Hey, girl. How's the mommy-to-be feeling?"

"Well, let's see. I'm packing up a house with nowhere to put anything, and my husband is losing his job. Oh, and my supposed best friend knew all along that my life was about to implode and didn't give me so much as a heads-up. How do you think I am?"

As the words bit through her, Minka kept a level head. "I deserved that. I'm really sorry, Lola. I all but begged him to tell you."

"Yeah, with an emphasis on *all but*."

"He's my superior. I have limits. I couldn't even talk him out of calling WITSEC on my husband or having my brother arrested."

"But I'm your friend. You don't have those limits with me. If I could've given you warning in those situations, I wouldn't have hesitated. If I had kept quiet, your reaction wouldn't be any better than mine."

"I appreciate that, but Gus is my friend, too."

"Just like Wes is mine," Lola said.

In an unsolvable conundrum, Minka rubbed her aching forehead. "I was just in a bad position. Please, understand that. I want to help you guys get through this."

"Sorry, Minka, but your time to help has passed, and I don't understand it. I'll tell you if I ever do."

With that, the call ended, as Lola hung up on her. Halfway home, Minka cried, devastated over the pain of losing two friends and a beloved commanding officer. She should've told Lola the truth, not to prevent their falling-out, but because it was the right thing to do. She deserved to be looped in on what was happening in her husband's life, especially with her already changing circumstances. Even so, all the blurred lines clouded her vision at the time, and she still wasn't certain she would've done anything differently if she had it to do over.

Her inner struggle overtook her whole night, not making for the best of times with her family. She was touchy with both Wes and Caela, and when he questioned the reason behind her short temperament, she ignored it. A good night's rest eluded her yet again, so she didn't rouse in a much better mood the next morning. Instead, she forced her fever-free daughter back to school in spite of her countless whines.

Of course, Renee's constant frown didn't help, nor did the surly expression on Gus. Before the day even began, she wished she could either sleep through it or spend it on the beach with a Mai Tai in hand. She was where she needed to be, though. Even with the sad state of her relationship with the Channings, she maintained her resolute determination to fight for Gus's job.

In keeping with that, her first task of the morning was to call the martial arts studio, in hopes they'd be open and able to tell her the name of Chandler Turner's dad. Nobody answered the phone, much to her aggravation. Logging back onto their social media page, she clicked on their hours to learn that if they did open, it wouldn't be until seven that night.

Minka groaned in frustration. "You can't be serious. We're losing an entire day of trying to crack this."

"That's the way it goes. If you ask me, I don't think it's really worth the hassle. I mean, I agree there's a resemblance between Everett's friend and that guy, but it isn't definitive enough to excite me. Yeah, he has the same hat and face structure, but so does Dawson Michaels, who you've conveniently scratched off as a suspect this whole time."

Minka didn't like the sound of the remark. "What are you implying?"

"The obvious. The man works across from the scene of the crime and had the prime suspect in front of his diner, talking to a guy in a hat from his son's class. With anyone else, you would deem all of those coincidences suspicious. Because of your attachment to him, however, you haven't even considered he could be involved."

"Attachment? I'm married, and I haven't run into him in fourteen years. Besides, if he was Everett's friend, why would he point out the logo to us? I can't speak for you, but there's no way I would've recognized that."

Renee crossed her arms and began profiling him, despite her earlier instructions to leave that to the feds. "Maybe he likes the thrill of the hunt. Give us just enough to lead us in the right direction and anticipate whether or not we'll catch him. Deep down, we all have an adrenaline junkie in us, and that's why we chose this career."

"I chose this career to help people, not lock up innocent ones."

"You have to follow due process to decide their innocence, Minka."

Astonished that her morning could actually get worse, she conjured up one last line of defense. "He had an alibi, remember? He said he left work before the blast. I'm sure I could use the surveillance to prove it."

"You're welcome to try."

Minka accessed the file and masked her relief when the footage showed Dawson unloading a delivery and departing almost forty minutes before the bombing, just as he claimed. When she presented it to Renee, she had to repress a chuckle at her indignant eye roll. Once it passed, her befuddlement set back in, as she debated where to go from here.

After she closed out the security footage, the Young Masters Martial Arts Division's page appeared again, so she decided to scroll through it. The afternoon before, she'd been focused on finding the man who was with Everett and had ignored most everything else. Now browsing in general, Minka's gaze landed on a photo of Chandler Turner and his fellow students, along with their instructor, Master Chuck Tsukino. Assuming he'd have insight into his student's father, she researched his phone number and address.

When she started to dial, her partner asked her, "What are you doing now?"

"I located Chandler's trainer, so I'm hoping he'll be able to tell me his dad's name. I understand your feelings, but my gut tells me I need to go after this."

"Suit yourself."

She ignored Renee's condemning manner, but the

all Japanese greeting on Master Tsukino's voicemail just about sent Minka's frustration over the edge. Grimacing, she didn't bother to leave a message. "Guess I'll have to make a visit to his house and hope he either has a translator there or knows ASL for some crazy reason. At the very least, maybe he can communicate to me who this guy really is. Are you sitting this one out or riding along?"

"It's been a long week. I suppose I'll mind the fort for a change."

"Fine by me," Minka nearly retorted. She welcomed the solo mission, in desperate need of an hour or two on her own. She wouldn't have to contend with the awkward conversations or unsettling silence in the car. Taking full advantage of it, she bumped up the radio's volume as many decibels as she desired. Like she always joked, she was already deaf, so what damage could it do?

Fifteen minutes into her jam session, her phone vibrated beside her. Her stomach churned when she read Gus's name. She couldn't have anticipated what he was about to say.

"There's been a bomb threat to Ryan and Caela's school!"

Chapter Eight

Minka bolted for the elementary school. Once she arrived, the scene filled her with terror. Five police cars, two fire trucks, an ambulance, and the bomb squad vehicle occupied the parking lot. The children had been evacuated to a nearby park, and many were already reunited with their distraught parents. As a mom, Minka yearned to rush over there and squeeze her little girl tight, but assured that the staff was keeping Caela safe, she forged ahead to do her job.

She raced up to Gus. "Is this Everett's doing?"

"It would appear so, but we honestly aren't sure. All we've ascertained is a guy called the school and claimed to have put a bomb in a locker."

"But they don't have lockers."

"Apparently, the higher grades do," he stated of the K-5 building. "The squad's sweeping the whole fourth and fifth grade wings."

She glanced toward the park. "Have you gone over to see Ryan?"

"No, I haven't had the chance. I don't need Friedman having that to use against me. Lola's on her way."

Not wanting to make matters worse for him, she followed his lead and refrained from venturing over to check on Caela. She caught sight of Cael, Declan, and Renee stationed beside a nearby patrol car, sharing the same anxious expression, and decided to join them. The detectives peered at the building in silence for what seemed like an eternity, before the bomb squad emerged, giving a very welcomed all-clear sign.

Nearly bursting into sobs over the relief, Minka hurried to find her daughter. To her relief, she spotted her almost right away, with Lola and Ryan standing beside her.

Her daughter jumped into her arms, a brave smile across her face. "I told everyone that my mom and uncle were going to catch the bad guys!"

Wishing they had, Minka only grinned, before— albeit apprehensively—she shifted toward Lola. "Thanks for staying with her."

"Of course. I'm sorry about yesterday."

"Me, too."

After the two hugged, Gus and the school's administrators arrived and announced that the kids would be released to their parents for the rest of the day, given the trauma they'd undergone. The decision posed a problem for Minka, as she again had to choose between her daughter's best interests versus those of her job. She debated the issue for a moment, until Lola asked if she wanted her to take Caela home to her house.

"I'm guessing we don't get the afternoon off, too?" she half-jokingly asked Gus.

"Not by any means. In fact, the school's agreed to have us stay here and dig through surveillance and whatever else we need to discern who made the threat."

"Couldn't it have just been a lunatic, calling it in from his recliner?" Renee said. "We have no proof they were even here, do we?"

Gus shook his head. "No. The call was untraceable, but we can't take anything for granted. Whoever did this knew there were lockers, so I'd say he was familiar with the building's interior."

"Unless it was simply a generic assumption," Cael replied.

Gus acknowledged the point, before he addressed Minka's quandary. "We could cover our bases here, if you need to be with Caela."

She squatted down in front of her little girl. "Do you want to go home with Mommy or Auntie Lola?"

"Auntie Lola. Ryan says their guest room is completely empty now, and your voice echoes in there. We can have our own concert."

Minka couldn't fathom how unfazed the six-year-old was by the morning's events. She giggled and whispered to Lola, "Just when we thought they couldn't get any louder."

Lola chuckled, as Minka thanked her for her help and kissed Caela goodbye. The three ambled away, and her conscience reproved her for how she'd treated her blameless family that morning. That could've been her last conversation with her child, and she spent it arguing over Caela's natural inclination to miss school. Worse yet, she could've been spared all of this anguish if only she'd given into the girl's wish.

Cael's voice jolted her out of her haze of regret. "You okay, Minks?"

"I made her go to school today. She said she didn't feel good, but I wouldn't listen."

In a rare display of empathy, Renee patted her on the shoulder. "You can't spend your life beating yourself up about could've beens. Just be thankful she's safe now."

Judging by the somber cast in her eyes and cadence in her voice, Minka perceived she was speaking from experience, no doubt her daughter's killing. She supposed every parent faced guilt when losing a child, whether they were right there when it happened or half a world away. In that moment, she finally felt a connection to her partner, privy to her vulnerable side for the first time.

She couldn't ruminate on sentiments, however, with Gus wasting no time to instruct them on what to do next. While he headed back to the precinct, he enlisted Minka and Renee to compare surveillance footage with the visitor log to verify the guests' arrivals and departures. At the same time, they'd keep a look-out for any suspicious activity. For their part, Cael and Declan would begin interviewing the staff to determine what they'd witnessed or if they were aware of underlying matters that could've led to this.

Minka and Renee trudged back to the building and into the main office. Employing the secretary's assistance, the detectives peered through the entire week's recordings of the building's perimeter, indoors and out. As they matched the times and names to the log, nothing notable happened, until the camera captured an enraged man storming into the school the day before.

"Well, he certainly didn't sign in," Renee said.

After the heated exchange between the man and the vice principal escalated, Minka summoned the secretary to join them. "Who is this guy?"

She didn't have to give the footage more than a glance. "Marty Sanders. His kid, Mack, is a problem child, and he can't accept it. He's always accusing us of picking on the boy every time he gets disciplined. Of course, it could never be the precious angel's fault for throwing punches and stealing his classmates' lunch money."

"Did the kid attend school today?" Renee inquired.

"No, he was suspended yesterday for the rest of this week—which provoked the father's outburst."

Minka crossed her arms. "So, what better day to give the school a scare? He knows his son is safe."

"Maybe the apple doesn't fall far from the tree," Renee replied.

****

From consulting with the vice principal and Mack Sanders's homeroom teacher, all four detectives agreed his father was a likely suspect to call in the bomb threat. Thus, Minka and Renee tracked down his information and opted to commence their search at his workplace. En route to the building materials factory, Minka lacked the usual vigor she had when following a lead. She supposed it was because of her traumatic morning, but deep down, something told her more contributed to the lethargy.

She finally put her finger on it. "If this is our guy, what's the connection to Everett?"

"Who says there is one?" Renee replied. "This could be completely unrelated."

"Those chances just seem so slim, don't you think? I mean, two bombings in two weeks, and he's behind both of them, but not a third instance? It seems too coincidental."

"Copycats are nothing new to crime, Minka. Besides, it could be another extremist, protesting all of the sloppy police work again."

"Or just an irate father, who isn't willing to admit that his kid's real problem may well rest with him," Minka stated. "Whatever the case, he has to answer to me, not because I'm a cop, but because I'm a mom."

"I can relate."

Rounding the corner, they parked in the factory's lot and asked to meet with Marty Sanders. They found him constructing floor trusses, the manufacturer's biggest seller. While he was in good shape due to his physical work, at first glance he didn't appear to be overly aggressive. Rather, his quiet on-the-job demeanor seemed to be a far cry from the volatile guy they observed on the surveillance footage. When his supervisor called his attention to the detectives, he didn't squirm or manifest any anxiety at all.

"Mr. Sanders, I'm Detective Hart, and my partner's Detective Avery. I'm sure you heard about the bomb threat to your son's school?"

"Yes, my wife called and told me. I was glad to hear everyone's safe. It's a scary world when you can't put your kids on the bus with the assurance that they'll return in one piece."

"It sure is," Minka agreed, cringing inside over his meek front. "But we hear you were spared that heartache this time, at least. Your son was suspended yesterday?"

"He was."

"Well, let me just say how fortunate you are. I have a kindergartener who goes there, and this has been the most terrifying morning of my life."

"I can imagine. I'm very sorry, Detective." He sounded sincere.

Renee took over the interview. "In our investigation of the incident, we learned from several sources that you had quite a confrontation with the vice principal yesterday. Can you shed some more light on that?"

He nodded in apparent shame. "I'm afraid I lost control. This is Mack's second suspension of the year—his fifth overall—and one more will get him expelled. Now, I appreciate that he can be difficult, but I feel he has two strikes against him just by entering a room. He's an easy fall-guy, and I won't be happy if he's denied an education because of it."

"So, in other words, you're convinced the school has it out for him?" Renee replied.

"To a degree."

Renee's eyebrow shot up. "You ever think of doing something about it? Evening the score?"

He started to give an affirmative answer, before he appeared to deduce their implication. "Is this about today? Do you really think I would threaten a school of small children over my kid's behavior?"

"Can you blame us?" Minka stepped back into the ring. "We saw the surveillance footage, and your argument seemed pretty heated."

"It was a tense moment. My son's future is at stake, but I would never rob others of theirs because of that."

They couldn't dispute his argument, with no basis to believe it wasn't genuine. Thus, Renee switched from speculation to facts. "What time did you arrive at work today?"

"Eight thirty, on the nose. Ask any of these guys."

"May we see your call history on your phone?"

Marty handed it over. "Be my guest."

The list showed no outgoing phone calls to the school within the past month. For good measure, they checked the factory's phone records, as well, which also came up clean. Their business done, they returned to the precinct emptyhanded. The school had given them the rest of the week's surveillance on a flash drive but already told them there hadn't been any other disputes like the one with Sanders. All in all, the situation seemed more hopeless than ever.

On the way back, the two conferred over the phone with Cael and Declan, who were still at the school. Their interviews with the staff hadn't yielded much, and they didn't have any leads, either. Their heads hung low as they retreated to their desks, but the sight of Gus carrying a trash bag into his office made Minka's snap up.

Minka followed him in and closed the door. "Friedman can't count today against your countdown. Look at what we had to face."

Gus sighed. "Ironically enough, today gave him more leverage to toss me. He said, if I can't protect my child, I have no business protecting this city."

****

On her drive home, with the day's events taking their toll, Minka couldn't keep from breaking down. Just minutes earlier, she witnessed her commanding officer and friend leave his office and enter a world of unknowns for his and his family's future. He'd been one of the few to be at one precinct from his rookie days forward, and even a couple of days prior, Minka expected him to retire from there. She cringed when envisioning that time but figured it wouldn't occur for another couple of decades. Here, optics cut his tenure short. Worse yet, he didn't get the honorable farewell he deserved.

Nonetheless, he handled his untimely departure with dignity, giving one final speech to his officers. He thanked them for the respect and loyalty they'd shown him over the course of his career, and—his gaze on Minka—he encouraged them to show the same to his successor. He concluded by expressing what a privilege it'd been to serve with them all, before shaking hands and taking his leave. Meanwhile, Minka had to conjure every morsel of her strength not to start sobbing then and there.

In the confines of her car, though, she indulged in her sorrow, without the restrictions of her own pride and professionalism binding her. She unleashed the conflict that'd been building inside of her ever since her return to work and even pulled off the road for a moment until she regained her composure. The torrent of emotions helped her to a degree, but it didn't make her any more eager to face the next day without Gus at the precinct.

Upon arriving home, Minka resolved to conceal her pain, not wanting to give Wes or Caela the wrong impression about her devotion to them. As much as she cared for Gus, coming home to them would always be her priority and the thing she couldn't bear to live without. It'd been jeopardized twice in the past three days, and she was beyond grateful that they were still together.

If she had any problem setting aside her concerns, the burden was greatly lightened when she stepped out of the car to find the contents of Caela's bedroom scattered across the backyard. Not to her surprise, her husband appeared to be the ringleader of the shenanigans, carrying a load of her stuffed animals. Meanwhile, the little girl trailed behind him, sassily scolding and wagging her finger. "This isn't funny anymore, Daddy!"

"What's going on here?" Minka questioned.

"Hey, honey," he greeted with ease, acting like he was in the middle of a routine task. "Our daughter was having such a fun time in an empty room at Lola's house, so it hit me: why spend all this money on toys and furniture and deprive her of the thrill of a bare room?"

Perceiving his methods to brighten the mood, Minka couldn't help but play along. "Makes sense to me."

"But, guys, I need somewhere to sleep and keep my clothes." Caela pouted. "And I really like my toys."

"That's true, too, Daddy," Minka said.

She anticipated him to indulge the impish child in him and carry the charade a tad longer, but the man who lived with two females seemed to persuade him to concede. "Fine, I guess you can keep everything."

Caela celebrated her victory, before another idea took form. "Since my room's already empty, though…"

"Go, have fun." Wes kissed the top of her head. Once she retreated into the house, he explained what his wife already understood. "I figured she could use a distraction after this morning."

"I caught onto your scheme. That's one of the many things I love about you." She kissed him and snuggled into his chest. "Truth is, I needed one, too."

"So did I. I about lost it when you called and told

me what was happening. Our little girl, Minka."

She couldn't say a word at first, his uncharacteristic expression of grief enhancing her own. Eventually, she swallowed hard and voiced what she'd been grappling with the whole day. "This is all my fault."

"What? How?"

"Everett warned us."

"You think this was an affront to you personally?"

She led him over to sit on the patio's couch. "I'm not positive, but I can't rule it out. We haven't linked a connection to him, but that doesn't mean there isn't one. Let's face it: the guy all but threatened us two days ago, and then, this happens. How can I not take it as a message?"

Wes's eyes revealed his alarm. "If that's the case, it means he has some insight into our lives."

"I was trying not to go there. To imagine a wanted terrorist is watching us—it's too terrifying."

"It is. Maybe he knew Ryan attended there, too. Go after a detective's daughter and a lieutenant's son at one time. It's efficient, for sure."

Minka seized the opportunity to break the news to him. "Make that an ex-lieutenant. Friedman cut him loose this afternoon. He told him if he can't keep his own child out of danger, he can't protect the city, either."

"You're kidding me. Give the poor guy a break."

"He just viewed it as a chance to boot him out, and he took it."

"But why? Gus has been devoted to that precinct for over a decade. How could he be so eager to get rid of him?"

She shrugged. "Politics, according to the office grapevine. With the mayor's recent election, Friedman has to be asked to stay on by him. The bombing alone has called it into question, so I guess this may be his Hail Mary. I just hate the prospect of starting over. A month ago, it excited me, but after this case and Renee, I realize what a creature of habit I am."

They sat in silence, which enabled them to hear rustling around the corner. With all the conjecture about Everett's insights into them, Minka's hand landed on her gun. Her fear gave way to annoyance when Camille appeared, eyes widening the moment she spotted the bedroom furniture on the lawn. "What is going on over here?" she cried.

Not missing a beat, Wes explained, "Caela missed a rent payment."

****

Gus's release was the top story on the evening news, with the media and Chief Friedman painting it as the best move that could be made. While the report acknowledged Gus's decorated career, the primary focus was, of course, the bombing investigation and the department's inability to capture Everett. Sickened by it, Minka went to change the channel but stopped when the anchor introduced a clip of the chief's press conference earlier that evening.

Friedman read the opening remarks of his statement right off his notes on the podium. "I understand that the suspect's remaining at large is not solely Lieutenant Channing's doing, as it isn't any of the other investigators'."

She wanted to gag over the hypocrisy of his words and the cavalier way he addressed firing a decorated officer. His cheesy smile sickened her, too, but she didn't like the glare he shot at the camera when he raised his head.

He didn't consult his notes any longer, making dramatic gestures during the denunciation that ensued. "At the same time, his mismanagement of his team has put the search in unnecessary danger, in my opinion. For instance, I recently learned that evidence indicates another party's involvement in the bombing. The lieutenant and his detectives decided not to put forth this theory even to me but opted to leave it to chance. In the meantime, this accomplice enjoyed his freedom to perhaps plan his next attack. Whether or not that would be today on a school full of innocent children, we can only guess."

Wes's mouth agape, he managed to speak Minka's thoughts before she could gather them. "How did he find out about your suspicions?"

"I don't have a clue. I shared my thoughts with Gus the other day, but he would never tip off the brass like that. The only one I confided in, besides you and Cael, is Renee, and she was completely on-board with keeping it hush-hush. I followed her lead, in fact."

"Don't get ahead of yourself, babe. Maybe one of them had a crisis of conscience." When she leveled an accusatory scowl his way, he jumped to his own defense. "I would never betray you like that. Man, woman, you are wound tight."

"I'm sorry…but my hide's on the line here, too. Whoever clued him in on the accomplice theory probably admitted I'm the one who thought it up. Judging by his dictatorial manner, I expect a write-up, at least."

"He hasn't contacted you so far, right?"

She shook her head, until her phone serendipitously began to ring. When she saw the caller ID, she released a cleansing breath. "It's Cael."

Her brother-in-law joined the debate as soon as she answered. "Did you spill the beans about Everett having a partner?"

"No, I told Gus my suspicions, but I doubt he did. Renee's the one who suggested we sit on it, but now, I'm starting to wonder if she spilled to IA without giving me the heads-up."

"I wouldn't be surprised," Cael said. "In her short time here, she's never seemed to be a big fan of Gus. I think it's because he's younger than her...and her commanding officer."

"It doesn't take much to get on her bad side. She wouldn't go on a lead with me today because she deemed it useless."

"I wondered where you'd gone this morning," Cael said. "Was she proven right?"

"I don't know. I was halfway there when Gus called about the school."

As Minka recalled the sequence of events, a disturbing notion materialized. She opened her mouth to relate it, but she couldn't summon the strength to confront it.

Still, the troubling notion didn't subside and continued to plague her hours later.

****

Despite her trepidation, Minka dragged her body out of bed the next morning and began her new reality. Chief Friedman sent out a group message the night before that instructed everyone to report Saturday to meet their new interim commanding officer. The prospect of reporting to anybody other than Gus hadn't yet fully absorbed, but she continued to remind herself that she'd wanted to be a cop long before she met Gus. Her reasons for being one ran deeper than being under his command.

Still, she doubted she would've ever earned the chance without him in her corner. As she drove to work, nostalgia struck her again, taking her back to the day she found Claire.

Minka's journey to Claire's supposed meeting place took longer than she anticipated. The landscape around her grew more remote with each passing mile, making her anxiety rise. She'd never ventured this far out of the city, so she had to depend solely on her GPS, which didn't always prove as reliable as the makers— and her dad—purported it to be.

At last, the box announced that she'd arrived at her destination, but the vacant lot didn't offer much to identify it. She scanned the surrounding area and recognized the nearby curve in the road along with the woods to the west. Foliage cloaked the property more than the aerial image portrayed, but in the distance, she noted the building that had beckoned her attention.

She drove down the dirt pathway, and the sight of a small blue car added to her worry about getting stuck. Her unease suddenly yielded to exhilaration when the *Georgia Girl* bumper sticker revealed it to be Claire's. Minka had passed it countless times in the parking lot. Right before she celebrated her victory, fear set in as she wondered why Claire would've stayed there for days. Her instincts told her that her neighbor didn't make the decision willingly.

Nearing the structure, she found it bigger than it seemed overhead, and it proved to be an old schoolhouse. She stepped out of her car and wandered closer, climbing the stone stairs that led to its oak door. The lock and chain around the handle appeared newer, showing no signs of wear other than a few scratches around the keyhole.

Locked out, she weighed how to proceed. The presence of Claire's car indicated she was there, but what could Minka do? She worried someone would report her trespassing if she created a ruckus, but she couldn't abandon her mission without checking the premises for her. Detective Channing's admonition to take along backup rang in her brain, until another cry muffled it. Spinning in the direction of the noise, she caught sight of Claire in the narrow window.

"Help! Minka, I'm here!"

Minka shuffled down the steps, frantically strategizing, and retracted her gun from its holster. She motioned toward the window on the opposite side of the entrance and drew a deep breath, having never used the weapon outside of the firing range. She shot three bullets into the window, making the glass shatter, and Claire leapt out of it at her command. She rushed into Minka's outstretched arms.

"Who trapped you in there?" Minka asked.

"The subject of an exposé I was writing—Captain Roger Detwiler."

The memory sent chills through Minka even now. As much as she resented her commanding officer, she never suspected Detwiler of being dirty.

Taking the exit that led to the precinct, she shifted her focus to her current case, but her drive to solve it waned. For the first time in many years, she concluded she'd failed, unable to catch a terrorist and his partner, bring justice to the city, and save her friend's job. She supposedly blew the whole investigation and may well have cost Gus his career. The burden a heavy one to bear, she struggled to rise above it and forge on with her work.

And if all of that wasn't enough, there was always the dread of facing another day beside Renee. While she analyzed her from afar when she arrived at the precinct, her partner seemed to be going about her morning as usual, unfazed by the prior day's events. Minka still wondered whether or not she tipped the chief off about Everett's partner. In spite of her temptation to ask, she honestly didn't want to verify it. Confirmation would only worsen their relationship, which was sure to run Minka off the force for good. Hence, she trotted over to her desk and tried to treat her like nothing had happened.

Renee's opening words didn't make it easy. "Ready to meet the new boss?"

"Sure," Minka replied, not needing any additional drama.

"From the way he worded the message, I gather Chief Freidman's going to pay us a visit, too," Renee said. "While I haven't appreciated his conduct around the press, I agree this place needed some shaking up."

"If only you'd fall off in the process!" Minka wanted to say.

She had weightier concerns, however, threatened by Friedman's visit. His words from the previous evening rang through her head, primarily the insolent tone when he said, "the lieutenant and his detectives decided not to put forth this theory even to me."

She couldn't help but worry over how he would treat her, certain he was aware of her role in that theory.

Before her imagination took over, the entire room began to stir with the entrance of Friedman and a man appearing to be around his age. The chief maintained the persona he manifested at his press conferences, serious yet donning a phony grin to make his listeners believe he was a friend.

"Good morning, Officers. I'm sure everyone's heard by now about Lieutenant Channing's departure. He's a good man and has served this department well for many years, creating strong bonds with most of you. That said, these last few weeks have exposed a need for a change, and I hope this will prove to fill that. I understand it may be a rough transition period, but to help us through that, I've called in a buddy of mine who recently retired from the Tampa department, Captain Rick Montgomery. He's excited to serve with you all until we hire a permanent replacement. Would you like to say a few words, Rick?"

The man stepped up and proceeded to give a brief synopsis of his life and accomplishments, along with his longtime affinity for Orlando. Mentioning his history in the military, he encouraged them to view every day as a battle, especially with the trauma the city had undergone. Despite the speech's motivational tone, Minka couldn't focus on much of it, her gaze drifting to Friedman the entire time. While he beamed at his friend with pride, she caught him stealing an occasional glance her way. His political poker face revealed no more. She tried her best to brush it off and believe she imagined it, but her stomach filled with apprehension.

After the group gave Captain Montgomery a round of applause, he retreated to Gus's former office, accompanied by Friedman. Noting their chumminess, Minka considered whether he'd staged this ruse all as a way to get his friend a second job. Maybe the freedom of retirement and the pension it provided didn't offer the sort of lifestyle Montgomery imagined. Bitterness bubbled inside her, liable to explode at any time, so she stopped her spiraling conspiracies from spreading any further. Speculation wouldn't change anything. Instead, she focused on her day, starting with trying again to make contact with Chuck Tsukino.

Just like the morning before, her plan was sidelined, this time by Chief Friedman approaching her and Renee. He cleared his throat, and his lively veneer lost some of its shine. "Detectives, Captain Montgomery and I would like to speak with you in private."

Minka and Renee obliged, netting many stares in their direction. Surely, everyone tuned into his press conference, and as the bombing's lead detectives, they'd be first in line to get reprimanded. Minka did her best to carry on with grace, but inside, agony ripped through her. She feared her childhood dreams of wearing a police badge would be dashed in the space of a few moments.

When she entered the room, she wasn't enveloped by the comfort it exuded when Gus occupied it. Stripped of the lieutenant's personal touches and the man himself, the bare walls felt isolating and intimidated her among this roomful of strangers.

After the four sat down, Friedman wasted no time, diplomatically stating, "Let me start off by thanking you two for your dedication to this case. We can agree this has been a dark period, and I'm sure you've given the matter your best efforts."

"We appreciate your noting that, sir," Renee replied.

He gave her a nod. "In the spirit of trying to better our proficiency, Captain Montgomery and I have decided it's time to hand the courthouse case over to Cael Avery and Declan Schuster. I understand you've been consulting with them all along, so they shouldn't have difficulty furthering the investigation from this day forward."

Renee's eyes widened in astonishment, appearing taken aback by the change. Minka maintained her wits and questioned him, "What would lead you to this decision? We've been working on this day and night. Nobody wants to catch this jerk more than we do."

"I'm aware of that, Detective. As I mentioned to the media last night, I don't hold it over anyone that Everett hasn't been detained. That said, I was unimpressed to learn that you weren't forthcoming about his having a partner. That was vital information the rest of the department, the FBI, and the public needed to be alerted to, so they could keep all methods of intelligence and apprehension open."

"But we weren't sure who it is—or if there really is a partner," Renee said.

Friedman leaned forward in his seat and tapped his finger against the desk, underscoring his authority. "That's not the point, Detective Hart. My problem is you withheld information, even from me. In an investigation of this magnitude, I consider that a serious concern. So serious, it was a key contributor to your

CO's being fired, and you're fortunate I'm not going to take similar action against you. Instead, I'm merely taking you off this case, and you're welcome to focus your efforts on others."

His decisiveness clear, the women regarded each other in silence and rose from their seats. Before they headed out the door, though, Friedman asked Minka to stay behind. With her nightmare unravelling, she sank down, still not uttering a single word.

"Detective Avery, we may have never met," Friedman began, "but you've always intrigued me, as you have many in the city. Yours is a true underdog story—a deaf detective, the lack of one ability balanced out by skills in police work. Gus Channing was your biggest fan from the very beginning. As you'd imagine, I was hesitant both times he recommended you, but he championed your case until I couldn't refuse."

His words sowed tears in Minka's eyes, especially since she could predict the outcome of his speech. "With all due respect, things are changing around here, and you're not exempt from that. Channing's gone now, and you have to prove your worth like everybody else. We don't keep officers on duty simply because of popularity."

His cutting threat pierced the depth of her very essence. "I suppose your history and friendship with Captain Montgomery didn't factor into your selection for our interim commanding officer, did it?" she scoffed.

The men exchanged sly grins, before Friedman sent a counterblow. "We'll let that one slide, Captain, and assume the detective couldn't hear what she was saying."

Chapter Nine

With her mind fixed on Freidman's scathing remarks, Minka trudged through her day in a haze. She didn't understand how he could expect anyone to go about their work with ease after such a beginning, but she tried to be resilient. She didn't confide in Renee or even Cael about the conversation, slightly afraid of their reaction. She couldn't decide what to make of the chief's words, wondering if he was threatening her job or trying to motivate her to do it better. Had he really been skeptical of her abilities from the get-go? Or was he like Captain Detwiler in Atlanta the whole time, viewing her as a cop but in name only?

She didn't have the answers; in truth, she couldn't say she wanted them. Her self-esteem plummeted to an all-time low; it affected her work performance, as hard as she tried not to let it. Since Freidman hadn't specifically barred them from investigating the school's threat, she and Renee scoped out leads, but she kept making sloppy mistakes. They ended their day early, given they were off the bombing case and didn't have reason to work on a Saturday.

Once home, she put forth a concerted effort to escape her concerns at the precinct and enjoy her family. Even so, she wasn't very talkative, but thankfully, Caela compensated for it. She had much to share about her day's adventures with her fun-loving dad, with whom there was hardly a dull moment. Still, his playful nature didn't supersede his perception, and Minka could tell he sensed her reserved behavior. He joined her in the kitchen while she cooked dinner and mentioned Cael texted him that morning during her one-on-one with Freidman and Montgomery. She didn't take the invitation to talk, aware it'd entail a deeper conversation than she wanted to delve into right now.

After they tucked in Caela later that night, she noted the suspicion painted across his face as he asked, "Any breaks in the case today?"

"I don't know. You'll have to ask Cael."

"He took it over? He didn't tip me off on that one."

"He didn't learn of it until after the chief and our new CO chewed me out. They reassigned it to him and Declan. I'm on their watch list and apparently am incapable to handle such a weighty investigation."

Wes lifted his brow and entreated her to elaborate. As she proceeded with her account, he comforted her without a word, tenderly rubbing her shoulder as they relaxed on the sofa. After she finished, he tried to reassure her. "You're not just an underdog tale. You've fought for and earned each of your accomplishments, deaf or not. His criticism says more about his character than yours. Now that his buddy is your superior, you can prove your worth to them both."

"But what if he uses Montgomery to keep stripping my cases from me and seal my coffin for good? It's the same issue I faced in Atlanta. Detwiler was never going to see my potential as long as he kept me at a desk with bogus assignments like proofreading reports."

"Don't get carried away, babe. It's only one case, and I'm big enough to admit that I hold a pinch of accountability for suggesting you keep mum on Everett's partner."

She playfully smacked his leg. "Just when I'd thought it'd plateaued, your maturity grows a little more every day."

They shared a brief chuckle, before Wes's curiosity kicked in again. "Were you at least able to find out about that karate fighter's dad?"

"I passed the information onto Cael, but he isn't allowed to talk to me about it."

Wes kept quiet at first, but before long, a devilish smile spread across his lips. Without a word, he seized his phone and video-called his brother.

"What are you doing?" Minka asked while they waited for Cael to answer.

Before her husband could respond, Cael accepted the call. His hand covered his eyes. "Tell me you are not in the bathroom!"

"Not this time, but if I were, it'd only be because I'm a busy man with little spare time to call my kid brother."

"And completely disgust him," Cael added.

"That, too. But tonight, I'm calling on my wife's behalf. She just gave me the lowdown on the madness at work and how you've taken the case."

"It stinks, man. It wasn't my call."

"I don't doubt that. I would just like to point out a loophole. Friedman says you can't talk to Minka about any developments, right?"

Cael nodded. "Afraid so."

Giving them both a mischievous grin, Wes proceeded to hold up his free hand and sign, *We have ASL. Problem solved.*

Minka didn't celebrate his cunning suggestion. "Come on, Wes. I'm in deep enough trouble, as it is."

"Yeah, an insubordination charge is all we need right now," Cael agreed.

"Suit yourselves."

The brothers briefly chatted about their week and plans for the remainder of the weekend, during which Minka contemplated her husband's devious strategy. As time elapsed, she began to take a liking to the proposition, actually wishing she'd cooked it up earlier. She stayed quiet up until Cael started to end the call.

She leaned into the camera's shot to make her appeal. "Wait! I know what I said about Wes's idea, but could we, please, humor him once?"

"Humor him?" Cael replied.

She rolled her eyes. "Or me, a little, I guess."

He agreed, and Wes angled the phone toward her. *Did you find out who Chandler Turner's dad is?*

His name's Clark Turner, and he and his family moved to Oregon five months ago.

She didn't hesitate to consider a follow-up. *Did Master Tsukino recognize the man with Everett?*

Cael shook his head. *The picture was too grainy. He admitted he doesn't have great eyesight.*

She sighed, dispirited even more. "You could've just told me it wasn't worth disobeying orders."

"Yeah, bro, call us when you have something juicy to sign," Wes instructed.

After he hung up, she kissed his cheek. "I love you, but I take back the maturity compliment."

He chuckled. "Stop pretending you didn't marry me because of my immaturity!"

****

After their conversation with Cael ended, Minka became more resolute than ever to keep her focus off of work. With no leads to track down, she should enjoy her first day off since taking the job and appreciate Friedman's removing her from the case. She no longer had to spend every waking moment calculating Everett's next move or analyzing who could be his accomplice. Until the city's next big crime, she was free…or at least, that's what she told herself and Wes.

Deep down, she didn't believe a word of her liberation act and doubted Wes did, either. By Monday—if not sooner—she'd return to obsessing over a case that wasn't even hers. To counteract that, they decided to seize the moment and head over to Cocoa Beach the next morning, like they'd done on many weekends when they were newlyweds. The road trip, of course, didn't feature much romance, with a six-year-old running around, chasing pelicans and sea gulls. Still, the short break provided what they all needed. Although only an hour away from home, the concerns of the week quietly floated off into the ocean.

The family headed back to Orlando in the early evening. The pressures of everyday life slapped Minka the instant they opened the door. Due to the tumultuous week, she neglected the chores, which led to a cluttered house. Each of them had left their mark on the living room; Caela's toys and art supplies scattered the floor, Wes's various snacks were strewn across the coffee table, and her array of shoes were piled high near the door. The stack of Judge Nichols's case files, however, stood out to the detective's eye the most.

Seeming like ages since she'd perused through them, she didn't long to resume her quest for clues.

During the weeks they'd been in her home, she made her way through most of them, with nothing to show for it but a couple of dead ends. At this point, she doubted the judge was ever a factor in the bombing. There were no connections between him and Everett, other than the brief time they worked in the same building.

She carried the folders and set them near the door to take to Cael and Declan the next day. She reflected on the hope they once held. When she first carted them home, she anticipated one would provide answers of who had done such a thing and why. On that line of reasoning, the realization struck her that, in their whole search for Silas Everett, they'd failed to determine his actual motive. True, his record of theft and subsequent firing from the courthouse flagged him as capable of decimating it, but was it honestly a valid reason for him to go to this extreme?

While she cleaned, she replayed the many developments in the investigation and recalled her theory that he'd merely been a patsy, with his partner being the real mastermind. She supposed whoever it was played on his bad history with the courthouse and threw enough cash at him to fund his life on the run. On the other hand, he had to realize this would be considered an act of terrorism. Would those two incentives be enough to take on that stereotype?

In this world, one never comprehended all of the aspects that triggered somebody to commit a crime, but as a detective, she wanted to nail down as many of them as possible. This may not have been her case anymore, but that didn't mean she wasn't a concerned citizen— who just happened to have a detective's training. Thus, after she finished straightening up, she typed his name into her laptop. This time, she didn't seek clues to lead her to his present whereabouts, but she sought indicators about his past that drove him to his current predicament.

The only child in his family, court documents revealed his parents divorced when he was seven, with his mother granted full custody. They both stayed off the record for the most part, until she was stabbed to death outside the grocery store where she worked. Before the days of top-of-the-line surveillance and DNA testing, police never solved the murder, but articles about the case alleged that her ex-husband was always suspected. Sixteen at the time, Everett filed for emancipation, no doubt to stay out of his father's custody and the foster care system. Shortly thereafter, he dropped out of high school and landed in juvenile detention within six months because of theft charges for stealing groceries. Ironically, he robbed the store where his mom was killed.

"The courthouse could hardly say they didn't see his sticky fingers coming," Wes said, reading the article over her shoulder.

"How long have you been back there?"

"Long enough to gather that you've already broken your oath to leave this in Cael and Declan's hands. But, please, don't let me stop you."

"Who says I would? Earlier tonight, I questioned whether or not we did enough homework on Everett to figure out his endgame."

"Well, you found it—the classic screwed-up childhood driving him to madness. Way to go, babe." He offered her a high-five, but her gaze didn't deviate from the screen.

"Thanks, I guess. I can't disagree with you, but what if there's more to it than that? Like with this, he probably was short on money and therefore food, but why from that store? If it were my mom's murder scene, I would avoid that place at all costs. Who's to say he didn't choose to steal from them because they, in his mind, failed to protect her?"

"Perhaps we've been watching too many of those crime series marathons."

She furrowed her brow. "Wes, I'm serious."

He plunked down beside her and sighed. "Okay, but where are you going with this? The robbery happened almost twenty years ago."

"I know, but what if he had the same motive in the bombing? What if he was convinced they failed her, too, maybe by not bringing her killer to justice?"

"Was she killed in the area?"

Minka skimmed through the article. "No, they were living in Key Largo at the time. Orange County wouldn't have been involved."

He patted her shoulder. "It was a nice shot, honey. I admire your diligence. On the same token, you should be punished for disobeying your chief's orders."

She closed her laptop and took the hand he extended to her. "Guess you'll have to put me in line, then."

****

Monday morning, Minka endeavored to embrace the new week with a fresh start. Sure, she grappled with the bitterness of Gus being gone and having the case snatched from her, but she had to remain professional. She vowed to tackle whatever arose and prove to Montgomery and Friedman that she was more than a popular headline.

She and Wes did their best to maintain normalcy with their daughter, as well, in order to help Caela face her first day back at school. The resilient little girl didn't seem to be too affected by the bomb threat, but they didn't want to take anything for granted. Minka remembered putting on an act of being fine in the months after Robin was abducted as a child, when she was suffering inside. Thankfully, the threat proved to be empty, but it still subjected the kids who were present that day to trauma.

At the school counselor's advisement, Minka and Wes took her to school, like the majority of the other parents. When they entered her classroom, Caela continued to behave as she did any other day, hugging them goodbye to indicate that she wanted them to leave. They had to chuckle on their trek to the exit, until they encountered Gus and Lola in the lobby. They hadn't talked since Gus's dismissal, so an awkward vibe lingered among them.

Ever the charmer, Wes initiated the conversation. "Good to see you guys. How was your weekend?"

"Quiet," Gus replied, which almost made Minka giggle because of their exchange the week before. "But productive. With my newfound free time, I can get most of the packing done on my own, which is better for Lola's sake."

Minka fought her curiosity about their plans, not wanting to add to their anxiety. "How's Ryan handled the bomb threat and everything?"

The parents compared notes on the kids, who both seemed relatively unfazed by the ordeal. Afterward, Wes had to get to work, having requested a substitute for only one class. Lola, whose baby bump now rose a bit more under her shirt, dashed off to the restroom, leaving Gus and Minka on their own. Minka realized she could—and probably should—depart for work, too, but she couldn't dart away from her friend like that.

"I'm sorry I haven't called since Friday. I just figured you might need some space," she told him.

"I appreciate it, but you don't need to worry about that. It feels like all I have is space right now...except for in my garage full of boxes." He let out a feigned snicker. "So, you like your new boss? I heard they finally booted out that old one you couldn't stand."

Minka shook her head, unsure how to reply. "The real question is does he like me. I'm afraid I have a ways to go on that front."

"Well, stick with it. You're an acquired taste."

"You're not the first one to tell me that," she admitted, smiling. Reminded of the chief's words about him fighting for her to be hired, she opened her mouth to express what that meant to her. Before the words emerged, however, she decided it was neither the time nor the place. "I'd better head over there now. Unpunctuality won't help my case with him."

He agreed, his expression kind, but she perceived his underlying pain. On the drive to the station, she had to dab away a few tears, nearly convinced that he wouldn't have lost his position if she hadn't gone back to the force. While the bombing wasn't her fault, she worried he landed on Friedman's cutting block because of his decision to rehire her. Friedman's dislike of her, as demonstrated two days earlier, seemed to run deep and not newly developed. She couldn't help but wonder on how many occasions Gus had to step up to bat for her and if that caused the tension between the two.

When she arrived at the station, she fanned her face and released a calming sigh. Cael arrived moments earlier, so she took the opportunity to hand off Judge Nichols's files. She related that she'd gained no insight into the bombing from them but entrusted it to his discretion on whether or not to return them to the judge. She resisted the temptation to mention her findings about Everett's mother, rationalizing that it led her nowhere the night before.

Nevertheless, her ponderings on Everett's motives circled her mind. Maybe it was a detective's keen instinct or simply her undying compulsion to break this case open, but she couldn't deem his past and present misdeeds unconnected. His mother's murder must have scarred him and could be the key to his current exploits.

Catching sight of the workload on her desk, she had to put her misgivings on the back burner for the time being. She and Renee revisited a couple of reports on cases that happened right after the bombing. Both being robberies, they'd recovered the stolen property and detained the thugs responsible. Though the thieves weren't acquainted with each other, they shared the same claim that they were so distraught by Orlando's woes, they needed extra cash to numb the pain.

"The things people do to play on your sympathy," Renee stated as she typed.

Minka agreed at first, reasoning as much while she reviewed them, but the spoken words took her back to her quandary about Everett. She already theorized that his cohort had played on his bitterness toward his ex-colleagues, but factoring in his troubled youth, she supposed he could've been manipulated in the same manner. Somebody who underwent an experience like his could have used that to strike common ground with him. If that were the case, it'd only make sense that the person had been let down by the Orange County Courthouse.

Mulling it over, Minka still couldn't decide whether or not she was truly onto something solid. Even if she was, it'd be a daunting quest to figure out who that person may be, assuming they didn't share any other connections to Everett. Numerous murder trials had occurred since the courthouse's opening in 1997; a fair amount ended without a conviction.

Over her lunch break, Minka typed *Orlando Murder Trials* into a search engine and couldn't believe it when the phrase netted over 150,000 results. Many articles discussed the same case, but the astounding list still painted a grim portrait of her family's hometown. She didn't have the time or mental stamina to weed through every single one, so she dismissed the idea and focused on her true responsibilities.

For the next several days, in fact, she suppressed any curiosity about the bombing and devoted her efforts to her other cases. Later in the week, she noticed an unusual amount of stirring on Cael and Declan's part, reigniting her interest. The fact that she couldn't ask about it frustrated her, but she quickly—and cunningly—realized she'd never reciprocated Autumn's hosting dinner a couple of weeks earlier.

With no plans that evening, they accepted her invitation to the impromptu family gathering. For the duration of their meal, Minka refrained from generating shop talk, except for when Autumn mentioned Gus and Lola's dire straits. Otherwise, they chatted about the kids, with Caela having started her new gymnastics class the previous night and little Tyson now beginning to stand against the furniture. After dinner, Autumn broke away to change his diaper, while Wes corralled Caela to finish her homework. With their spouses and children gone, Minka couldn't ignore the prime opportunity to corner her brother-in-law.

Any leads? she signed to him.

Cael cracked a grin. "I should've guessed your true intentions."

Well? she prodded. *I take it you haven't figured out who that guy in the martial arts cap was.*

No, he admitted. When she remained silent, he took a moment, evidently to consider whether or not to indulge her. In the end, he relented. *We returned to the feed store, and the owner recognized him as a customer. He's only shopped there a couple of times, and she doesn't know his name. She says he's always paid in cash.*

Did they have a surveillance camera?

He nodded, but his frown didn't transmit optimism. *We spotted a guy who stopped in the week before the bombing, and he wore the same hat. That's why she recognized him. Unfortunately, he kept his face angled away from the camera at all times. He seemed skilled in evading notice.*

Did he purchase ammonium nitrate? Minka asked.

Yes, but not in a big quantity. We're still trying to comb through the whole month of footage to catch another visit he made to determine if he bought a little at a time. If he didn't, Everett must've stocked up the brunt of their supply.

Minka paused, pondering the development. "I

should've thought to go back there. I began suspecting he had a partner the night after we met her. Maybe Friedman's right."

"Right about what?"

"Me, that I'm no detective. He implied I'm only a novelty act Gus believed in, which I'm guessing, contributed to his being fired."

Cael took a seat beside her. "Why are you playing the blame game with yourself?"

"This isn't a game, Cael. Ask Freidman. He'll tell you what a failure I am."

"And then, he can tell it to the media after I out him as a prejudiced idiot. I'd love to be front and center at that press conference."

She gave a half smile over his protectiveness. "He told me he never wanted me on the force."

"I doubt he wanted me, either, if he read the academy's full report on me."

Laughing, she locked eyes with him, and gesturing to the transmitter in her ear, she asked, "How can you act as though you don't see this?"

"It's no act; I don't see that. All I see is my friend, my sister-in-law, and the best detective I know—besides me, of course."

Minka played along, swallowing the lump in her throat. "Obviously."

"And if our dear chief can't realize that, I say he's the one with the handicap," Cael declared.

****

Cael and Autumn's visit reinvigorated Minka, and by the end of the night, most of her pent-up tension dissipated. Between Friedman, Montgomery, and even Renee at times, she'd grown to feel outnumbered and unappreciated, but Cael's kind words gave her a glimmer of hope. He boosted her confidence that things would eventually get back to where they were before she resigned. Of course, the precinct would never be the same without Gus at the helm, but she couldn't mourn his absence for the rest of her career. She'd just be satisfied if her superior would at least consider her as part of the team, rather than the player they let off the bench only long enough to strike out.

She figured that wouldn't happen, however, until they caught Everett and his partner and brought them to justice. Her thoughts drifted back to Cael and Declan's revelation about the mysterious accomplice, as well as her earlier strategizing about the possible goal he shared with Everett. She wished there weren't so many suspects who could have a bone to pick with the judicial system, and her heart sank again over the bleak fact.

With renewed resolve, Minka meandered over to her computer after putting Caela to bed. She searched through murder trials, but only from the past two years. Hoping it would result in less staggering matches, she shook her head when a six-digit figure still popped up. She decided to dig in, anyway. She kept an eye out for someone resembling the man in the photo with Everett or with a similar description who may have been connected to a victim. She estimated he was in his late thirties and stood nearly six feet tall. To her disappointment, she uncovered no such mention or picture.

Right before she opted to call it a night, a headline with her partner's last name beckoned her attention, and she clicked on it. Dated ten months ago, the article related the tragic story of Renee's daughter's death. As Cael told her, a collision with a drunk driver killed thirty-year-old Scarlett during her drove home on the interstate. The other driver was a congressman's son with two prior DUI convictions. The article claimed she'd spent the day wedding shopping, with her nuptials set to take place the next weekend.

The narrative quoted part of Renee's courtroom testimony. "Because of him, I have a wedding gown in my closet that I will never see my daughter wear down the aisle."

In the end, the jury ruled the defendant guilty of vehicular manslaughter, and the judge sentenced him with a meager community service order. The verdict was rather negligible, especially for a repeat offender, reportedly incensing the Hart family. They, along with the press, believed that his father's position and relationship with the court influenced the scales of justice. Scarlett's fiancé shouted and thrashed as the bailiff escorted him from the courthouse, and later that night, his mother checked him into the mental hospital.

Closing her laptop, Minka blinked away tears of sympathy for her partner, unable to imagine losing Caela, days before her wedding, to boot. She couldn't say she blamed her for being livid or even for her rigidness now. No parent could recover from a tragedy like that, let alone a woman who dealt with criminals on a daily basis.

The heartbreaking experience dominated her thoughts for the rest of the night and into the next morning. She wished she could talk to Renee about it, if only to express her condolences. She wondered how the family was coping, particularly Scarlett's fiancé. He obviously loved her very much and burying her close to—if not on—their wedding day would be anyone's nightmare.

All of a sudden, her sadness changed to intrigue, as she began to contemplate whether or not she stumbled on what she'd been seeking at the beginning of her web search. With Scarlett thirty at her time of death, her groom would've likely been around her age, putting him in the range of Everett's partner. He also fit the profile, embittered with the legal system and plausibly the courthouse, where the trial took place. His mental issues may have driven him to a criminal act, like they did to many other suffering patients.

Once the possibility occurred to her, she couldn't let it go, and even with other cases meriting her attention, she had to pursue the notion…beyond Renee's notice, of course. His name didn't appear in the article she read the previous night, so she had no choice but to investigate more about Scarlett. She skimmed through several other pieces on the woman's death and the trial, none of which revealed his name, before their engagement announcement identified him as Ivan Langat. The photograph that accompanied it answered Minka's curiosity, with him being a Kenyan native who bore no likeness to the man with Everett.

Her latest theory up in smoke, another wallop of frustration smacked her, and she admonished herself yet again to dismiss the matter. A stolen car was reported minutes later, which promised to serve as a welcome distraction. Both detectives rushed out, so fast that Renee forgot her car keys on her desk. Minka offered to retrieve them, given she was twenty years her junior. She ended up taking longer than her slower partner would've, though, because of the distraction that confronted her.

In their weeks of working together, she never felt welcome enough to examine Renee's framed family photos on her desk. Due to her recent peering into their lives, she couldn't fight the urge to pick one up and briefly study it. Taken at a wedding, Renee's family surrounded the couple, she at the groom's side, undoubtedly his mother. Scarlett stood as a bridesmaid, her joyous smile so contagious that Minka could barely avert her gaze from her. Because of time constraints, she couldn't peer any longer, but as she set it back down, she zeroed in on the groom and noted the distinct features.

Dark hair, cut close with sideburns. Rounded jawline. Approximately six feet.

With Scarlett appearing to be younger than him, he'd be in his late thirties by now, as well. All of it fell together, and the similarities between him and Everett's companion were undeniable. Even more, he, like his sister's fiancé, had motive to want vengeance on the court, an older brother's protectiveness at times fiercer than a lover's.

Renee's voice sent Minka's heart-rate spiking. "What's the hold-up here?"

Thrust into reality, Minka swiftly put the picture back before she could notice it in her hands and grabbed the keys in front of her.

"I'm sorry, but my phone started ringing when I came in, and I answered it in case it related to the grand theft. It was only Wes, though."

"Now wasn't the time to get chatty about your day," her partner said.

You're telling me, Minka thought.

Chapter Ten

Awkwardly trudging through the day, Minka grappled inside, weighing out whether or not her suspicion of Renee's son was more than a wild theory. She recalled Cael's point while they viewed the fight videos, that Everett's partner's attributes were fairly common. Plus, with how little the blurry photo revealed, it was difficult to narrow down anything that conclusively set him apart. As time passed, Minka supposed her dislike of Renee may have led her to such a rash conclusion, making her latch onto a piece of evidence that wasn't even there.

Still, she couldn't ignore how closely his experience with his sister mirrored what she'd guessed the bomber's motive to be. The trial didn't seem to be botched by a lack of evidence or an incompetent jury; rather, it was, to most onlookers, a biased scheme on the court's part. Thus, the oldest Hart son would've had plenty of reason to crave retribution, even more than Minka predicted the perpetrator would have.

Conflicted, she reasoned that, like she would do with any hypothesis, she could still research it. Assuming she handled it properly, she could use her relationship—if one could call it that—with Renee to grasp a perspective into her children's lives. Granted, Renee didn't manifest any interest in sharing personal details from the start, but Minka hoped that she could persuade her out of her obstinate shell.

"We let Caela enroll in gymnastics, and I can't believe how much busier it's made the week. The other night was just her first class, but getting her outfit and everything ready, besides helping her with her homework, made time vanish," she told her partner on their drive back from investigating the car theft. "I can't imagine how crazy your life was with three kids."

"It was hectic, especially in their later years. Thankfully, kindergarten wasn't what it is now. I don't recall them having homework assignments until at least the second grade."

The conversation showed promise, so Minka pressed further. "What are their names, again?"

"Liam, Ben, and Scarlett." Her voice cracked when she stated her daughter's name—not uncommon to parents who'd lost a child.

Since Renee had yet to divulge Scarlett's death, Minka treaded with discretion. "She's your youngest?"

"No, Ben is. He was our surprise. Liam and Scarlett were teenagers when I found out I was pregnant."

"Surprise is an understatement, if you ask me," Minka replied with a chuckle. She mentally noted that the groom in the portrait would've been Liam. "Were they close growing up, in spite of the age difference?"

"Yeah, they actually were. As odd as it sounds, Ben's late arrival strengthened the other two's bond. They'd started to drift apart at the time, but when I had him, they both wanted to be part of his life, so they ended up spending more time together again. They had sort of a second childhood, which was somewhat better than their first; they'd learned how to share by then."

"You're fortunate. My brother and I haven't mastered it, and we're in our thirties," she joked.

"The boys still have their moments, too," Renee admitted with a smile, continuing to withhold any details about Scarlett. "But Liam's a terrific big brother. He's always cherished his siblings."

The statement fell in line with exactly what Minka sought, but the taste of a lead lacked its usual sweetness. Instead, bitterness overwhelmed her, making her recoil inside. For the first time in her career, she had a glimpse into a suspect's human side. Rather than just a name, face, and potential motive, she was introduced to him as a loving child and brother. True, almost every criminal's loved ones endeavored to portray them like that, but it was typically in the context of a defense. By that point, an onlooker disregarded it and focused on the evidence. Since Renee didn't have the slightest idea of her partner's skepticisms, her account was sincere, no more than a mother's fond reminiscence.

Throughout the course of the rest of her afternoon, Minka's change of heart slowly convinced her not to act on her earlier thoughts against Liam. She resorted back to the rationale that she'd transferred her animosity toward Renee onto her family. Denouncing her spiteful tendencies, she deemed the conversation beneficial, not only to her covert investigation, but to their partnership.

Her newfound contentment apparently showed when she returned home from the precinct, with Wes saying, "Looks like somebody had a good day at work for a change."

"I did," she agreed, kissing him. "I think Renee and I are forming a connection. Today, we had a real conversation that didn't have to do with a case. I had to make the first move, but she reciprocated well. I wouldn't call her a friend yet, but I hope we're on our way."

"I'm glad to hear that, babe. I know how much having a good partner means to you. I'm happy to share the privilege of being your sounding board."

"Which, in the language of husbands, means, 'I'm tired of you talking!' "

"You're fluent in three languages now?"

She laughed and sat down at the dining room table to sort through their mail. Under a couple of bills and junk items was Caela's school's monthly newspaper, always a quick skim for Minka. Because of the bomb threat, she took her time with it, but the date in the corner revealed it'd been printed the day before the chaos. Even so, she gave it a thorough look-through for once to learn what her daughter would be facing in the upcoming weeks. She still flipped through it pretty fast, since many of the events and articles concerned the higher grades, but she paused when she made it to the last page. The headline seemed to be just for her.

Congratulations to Fifth-Grader, Jonah Hart, Our Red Belt Karate Champ!

The article praised the ten-year-old son of Liam and Tanya Hart, who was enrolled in none other than the Young Masters Martial Arts Division. Frantically reading on, Minka soon connected the dots: Liam had connections to both the karate studio and Caela's school, meaning he could be both Everett's accomplice and the one who'd made the bomb threat. With his son in fifth grade, he'd have experience with the older kids' lockers, where he claimed the explosives would be.

Her head spinning, she grappled with the question of why he'd do such a thing to his own child's school.

All of a sudden, the same nauseating idea she had the night after it happened struck her again—he called it in to divert her away from Master Tsukino. If she'd gone through with the meeting as she planned, his son's teacher may have recognized his picture, and he couldn't risk that. Of course, he'd need insider knowledge to learn of her morning agenda, and Minka didn't have to ponder it for very long to guess who'd give it to him.

Renee.

****

Barely able to process the enormity of her conclusion, Minka tried again and again to convince herself that she was wrong. Whether she liked any coworker or not, she'd never want to accuse someone of being a corrupt cop. She didn't enjoy their brief partnership—ironically, up until today—but this would affect far more than her. With all of the other hits the city and department had suffered, a scandal like this could derail their credibility altogether.

Unlike her theory of Everett's ally, however, she couldn't shy away from it for the sake of appearance. Rather, she'd pursue it and follow wherever her suspicions led. She chose to keep her suspicions from her outspoken husband this time. She waited until he fell asleep to revisit her research on Scarlett's death to hunt for more clues. Searching the police database, she dug up the accident report, which listed the date as February fifth. Her eyes almost slid over the detail, but her instinct forced her to concentrate on it. Employing all the brain power she could muster at two in the morning, she finally caught it.

Collector25, the username of whoever tried to buy the blueprints from Gill. The numbers did represent an anniversary like she suspected, the anniversary of Scarlett's crash. She called to mind her exchange with Renee about what the pseudonym may mean and remembered Renee's vague suggestion of it referring to a road. Did Liam still have her in the dark at that point? Or did she blatantly mislead Minka to her face?

Her memory of the day also conjured up the repeated occasions when Renee pressed for Gill to take the fall. After some scrutinizing, she concluded his alcoholic leanings may have put a target on him, as he would've reminded her and Liam of the drunkard who ended Scarlett's life. On a hunch, Minka searched his record, and the results listed two DUI charges. Both times, the court gave him the minimum penalty, in all likelihood because of his connection to Nichols. He already worked at the courthouse at the time of the second arrest, but he retained his job. None of it affected Renee's family, but the ordeal mirrored the injustice they witnessed, making Gill and Nichols prime candidates to take the collateral damage in their protest.

A flurry of instances where Renee probably manipulated her focus tumbled like dominos. She recalled the times when Renee hastened to conclusions even if the pieces didn't fit together. Her desperation to point the blame at Everett alone now made sense, as did her reluctance to admit he had a partner. She could've even planted the fertilizer in his SUV and engineered the vehicle to be impounded.

Minka pumped the brakes on her spiraling and opted to disregard the personal betrayal for now so she could focus on how to proceed. Given the magnitude of the accusation, she couldn't throw the theory out into the air and expect Montgomery to grant her unilateral permission to investigate. Even Gus would've given her push-back. Renee was a decorated policewoman who served the force for decades. Alleging she had a part in an act of terror would carry dire consequences, so she needed to have her facts straight and her evidence solid. While her discoveries were undeniably brow-raising, none provided a conclusive link between her and the bombing. Even Minka's case against Liam needed some indisputable proof.

Normally, she would've confided her theory in her partner so they could tackle it together, but she didn't have that option this time. True, she could approach her with her concerns, but given the fragility of their relationship, the scenario didn't offer much promise. Besides the tongue-lashing she'd receive, she feared what Renee might do to misdirect her again or worse yet, if she'd set Minka up to appear like the traitor.

Her debate continued into the morning, until she resolved that she needed to bounce the whole mess off of someone. Since her mind remained unchanged about not involving Wes, she offered to pick up a pizza for their lunch Saturday, choosing the parlor in Cael's neighborhood. With twenty minutes to kill while she waited for it to be prepared, she wandered over to his and Autumn's cottage. After all, as the case's lead detective, he should be informed of any leads or tips.

She found him mowing the grass when she arrived, which relieved her of the guilt that would've stung her if she'd interrupted his family time. She parked while he had his back toward her, so he flinched in surprise when he pivoted at the end of his row and spotted her.

He pushed out another row and shut off the engine once he made it to her. "What are you doing in this neck of the woods?"

"Waiting on our pizza."

Her claim incited a cynical frown on Cael's face. "From the place the health department shut down?"

She shrugged. "The exterminator handled it. Besides, I need to run something by you. Now, I realize it may sound a bit unbelievable, but at least hear me out."

She started with her insights into the death of Everett's mother and recapped the steps she'd taken over the past two days. Then, she voiced the conclusion to which they led her. She stated the facts as concisely and unbiasedly as possible, but in the end, Cael still took it to stem from her own ill will.

"Listen, Minks, I understand you and Renee aren't the best of friends, but you can't let it consume you to this point."

"This has nothing to do with my feelings for her. In fact, I was honestly starting to think things were improving between us yesterday. Ask Wes."

"So, was that before or after you decided her son is a terrorist?"

"In between." When he crossed his arms, she endeavored to level up her powers of persuasion. "This isn't my rage-induced decision, Cael. I don't want it to be true, but I can't ignore the signals, and neither should you. I should've perceived this sooner. On every lead we had that ended up to be a dud, she tried so hard to prove probable cause. Then, Dawson gave us the tip on the karate studio, and she wouldn't even go with me.

And you know why? Because she had to call her son to get him to threaten my kid's school!"

He crinkled his brow, a smile briefly flashing across his teeth before he contained it. "Nope, that doesn't sound a bit rage induced."

She groaned and paused for a beat to collect her composure. "Just set my feelings aside for a minute, and answer this: Why would Everett pounce on the chance to claim there was a crooked cop involved in this? Sure, we assumed he wanted to get revenge on us for using Peta, but does that really add up? He could've used Steward to convey any message he wanted. Instead of trying to deny he had any part in the bombing, he threw out the corruption card. Why?"

"Because that's up Steward's alley, and it'd generate the most buzz."

She couldn't argue with his logic, but she persisted in her plea. "You have to believe me on this one. If Renee is dirty, there's no telling how far she'll go. We may never catch Liam with her on his side."

"I'll keep me eyes peeled, but I can't make any promises with no true evidence."

She didn't like the response, but she reckoned she would've given a similar one if she were in the same position. They resorted to small talk for the next few minutes before returning to their separate duties. On her way back from the pizza parlor, despondency washed over her, with the excursion seeming like a wasted effort. While she appreciated having a second set of eyes on Liam and Renee, Minka doubted she'd convinced Cael of the validity of her claims. He'd be convinced her bitterness drove her theory, and she worried the notion would sap him of the zeal to give it thorough attention.

Nonetheless, she did her best to act like nothing happened when she arrived home and to be present during her time with Wes and Caela. She found it easy at times, like when they enjoyed a game of putt-putt later that afternoon. In the mundane moments of watching a show Caela had viewed countless times or when she did laundry, however, she struggled to maintain her focus. Deep down, she understood how outlandish her theory sounded, but even if it were partly true, the possibility that she may work alongside a traitor disturbed her.

As she observed Caela doing mazes the next morning, she imagined being in one of them, taking turn after turn that ultimately led to a wall. Caela slammed her fists on the coffee table, mirroring her mother's exasperation. Wily Wes crossed the room to offer a solution.

"Don't you notice that shortcut, honey?"

"What shortcut?"

"This one here," he explained, drawing a line from the start point, around the maze's border, and over to the end.

"What kind of teacher are you?" his wife asked.

"I'm teaching her to think outside the box."

"Yeah, I'll let you handle that argument at our next parent-teacher conference, Mr. Avery."

Despite her disagreeing with his methods, Minka couldn't stifle a slight chuckle. Not long afterward, his scheming struck a chord with her, similar to when he'd tried to manipulate their game of sleuthing. She had to start thinking outside the box again, the way she had on her first case in Atlanta as well as when she delved into the false assault charge against Robin. With both ending in good outcomes, she ought to tap back into her outside-of-the-force ingenuity.

In any investigation—under the radar or not—she had to exhaust all her resources, and Minka identified a vital one at her disposal. Dawson's son was enrolled in the same martial arts center as Liam's son, and she estimated that they could be the same age. Now armed with her suspect's name, she could get her friend's take on him. Granted, Liam probably wouldn't have spoken to him about the bombing or his disdain for the judicial system. Given his police training, though, Dawson may have a more perceptive read on his characteristics.

Naturally, she couldn't go and talk to him with Renee on this occasion. Being mid-morning on Sunday, Minka seized another ideal opportunity to entice her family with food in pursuit of a lead. The only hurdles she'd have to overcome proved to be her husband's taunting and her daughter's kind-heartedness.

"How would you two like to try out a new diner for brunch?"

"I assume you're referring to Dawson Michaels's diner." Wes said the name with the intonation of a teenaged girl talking about a heartthrob.

Before Minka could respond to his mocking, Caela asked, "Can we ask Uncle Cael and Aunt Autumn to come, too?"

"Don't you dare," she automatically cried. Her insistent tone elicited confused grimaces from the father-daughter duo. "I'm sorry. With Tyson's colic and teething, I just don't think he'd mix well with a busy restaurant. Besides, I doubt they serve vegan bacon for Aunt Autumn."

The little girl accepted the excuse and rushed upstairs to retrieve her shoes. Wes, on the other hand, didn't fall for it so easily.

He leveled a skeptical gaze at her. "Why don't you want Cael to know what you're doing?"

She grinned and gave him a playful peck on his nose. "Leave the detective work to me, honey."

They set off for downtown, and upon arriving, they discovered the eatery packed. Barely able to secure a parking space, Wes had to squeeze into the first one behind the building. The family circled it to get to the entrance, and not surprisingly, the line of customers awaiting a table filled the small lobby.

"It's seventy-five degrees and sunny, people! Let's eat outside." Wes gestured to the vacant tables outdoors. He winked at Minka, adding, "Unless that's a problem for you, dear?"

Truth be told, it was since she planned to chat with Dawson about Liam. Then again, she worried that a crowd like this wouldn't create the right atmosphere. Why risk losing her cover with her husband…and give him more ammunition?

"Not at all," she replied.

Seconds later, Dawson emerged from the kitchen, and after attending to a family seated in a nearby booth, he strode over to them. He shook Wes's hand and gave Caela a high-five, before Minka asked if they could take a seat outside. He gave them the go-ahead, so the three headed out the door. While they waited for their menus, Minka took in the scene around them, an eeriness welling up inside of her. Across from them stood the courthouse, with the damaged area still boarded up and under construction. Even worse, they sat in the very spot where Everett was pictured scheming with his partner. Although the general public didn't realize the latter, she figured the scene kept people from wanting to dine out there.

Continuing to contemplate the predicament, she peered over at the vacant century-old mansion beside them. She couldn't help but wonder if they should've investigated it further. They'd discussed it the day after the blast, but with no surveillance system to speak of or anyone there, they—especially Renee—dismissed it as a viable option. In retrospect, she regretted not digging deeper. The lack of occupants would've made it a conspirator's dream hideout, lending a prime view of the target. Robin's words drifted back into her mind about not being quick to write off a hideaway that seemed too obvious.

The possibilities mounting, Minka had to employ all her willpower to remain seated and not go over to scout out the property. Thankfully, Dawson's arrival with their menus kept her mind semi-occupied for the time being, but throughout their meal, her gaze kept drifting to the building. She caught a glimpse of a rustling curtain on the top floor, which nearly made her jump out of her skin. Her sudden movement took Wes and Caela aback, so she strived not to let her imagination run wild.

Not wanting to waste the opportunity to bend Dawson's ear about Liam, she took the bill inside to pay at the register after they finished their meal. With the dining room still pretty crowded, she'd have to be both discreet and brief.

In an effort to do just that, she handed him her credit card, and as he ran it, she casually leaned against the counter. "By the way, are you familiar with Liam Hart? His son, Jonah, takes karate at the same studio yours does."

"That kid's so good, he basically teaches it now." He wore a wide smile, until he seemed to catch onto the reason for her query. "I've only seen his dad from afar. Jonah's a year older than Kent."

"What's he like, from the little you can tell?"

"Pretty laid-back and reserved. He never screams at Jonah the way some other dads do, but then again, he usually doesn't have to because of the kid's skills. He always has a big circle of family around him. He seems like a nice guy."

Minka waited for him to recognize that her partner was among the supporters, but he didn't have such an epiphany. She thanked him for his input and the delicious brunch. Meanwhile, insecurities began rushing through her mind on her jaunt back to their SUV, as she questioned her speculations about Liam. If he really was so mild-mannered and likeable, could she really believe he was a vindictive bomber?

Studying the empty building beside them again, she wanted so badly to indulge in her curiosity. Her gaze wandered over the place, until she spied a small object in one of the windows. She took a picture of it with her phone and zoomed in on the image to try discerning what it was. She still couldn't draw a solid conclusion, but the round item sure resembled a security camera.

Minka surveyed her surroundings and envisioned the photo Everett leaked to the press. If her memory served, the vantage point of the picture aligned perfectly with the position of the assumed camera on the windowsill. Of course, it might be old and disconnected. If it was functioning and under Everett's control, though, it'd explain how he captured the meeting with his partner.

Wes, who'd headed to the parking lot while she paid, rounded the corner of the diner. "What's the hold-up?"

She almost asked his opinion about the object, but not liking to leave Caela unattended, she apologized and hurried along. She studied the photo she took as they walked and pondered whether she was growing overly suspicious. Right before she made it to the vehicle, she glanced over toward a gray crossover parked behind the mansion. She recognized a bumper sticker it bore, which propelled her conspiracy theories further. She tiptoed toward the chain-link fence that separated the properties for a closer look.

She gasped when she confirmed it to be the karate center's logo, just like the one on the cap of Everett's partner.

****

Before she ducked into the car, Minka speed-typed the license plate number into her phone so she could run it through the database on her laptop. She scrambled up the stairs with it the moment they returned home and locked the bedroom door, seizing her computer. She punched the seven digits into the search box and waited with bated breath. The result seemed to take an eternity to load, but it didn't disappoint.

Liam Hart, the screen read.

Bouncing on her bed like a kid, she grabbed her phone to pass the information on to Cael, but her better judgement stopped her. As much as she hated to admit it, this still didn't prove anything. Liam's car being there didn't mean he was a part of the bombing, especially with it taking place three weeks earlier. She couldn't place him there that night, and even if she could, his presence alone didn't implicate him in the crime. At best, they could only charge him for trespassing if he was, indeed, taking up residence there.

Moreover, his car being there didn't mean he was the one driving it. With Everett still off the radar, Liam might've lent him his vehicle, if he was his accomplice. They knew—whether from Renee's lips or the news—that he was spotted in the green van, so he could've swapped it out for another ride. The only part that didn't make sense was that, if he were so concerned with remaining out of sight, why would he hide only feet from the scene of the crime? Was he that much of an adrenaline junkie or just plain ignorant?

Back to Robin's point, however, one could call it a brilliant strategy, given it was such an unlikely place to look. Everyone expected him to have fled the county, at the very least. Plus, if Renee was on their side, he could safely stay almost anywhere, with the assurance she'd steer her colleagues away.

With that in mind, she recalled Everett's words to Peta about his escape plan and contemplated how much Renee factored into it. Considering her hastiness to pin the whole thing on him, Minka could imagine her and Liam withholding whatever they offered him just to keep him in the equation. The more attention he drew by staying close, the less likely they were to discern Liam's role. Renee probably didn't want her son to have to flee the area with his family, so the best course was to keep Everett as the carrot in front of the police. Only time could tell if she'd forever protect him or if she'd eventually betray him to conclude the investigation.

On the converse side, Everett's knowledge gave him leverage in the deal. He could expose Liam and derail her career in one fell swoop. He even proved that by leaking the photo to Steward. Maybe they'd wavered on their end of the bargain, so he decided to remind them of his power.

The entire situation eating her up, Minka hated the restraints that tied her hands. All she needed to do was go to the realtor who was selling it, show off her badge, and demand to have access inside. She doubted they would realize she was off the case, and she considered it improbable that the department would get wind of it. Even so, she feared taking that slim chance, with Friedman on her tail. He didn't need much of an excuse to seize her badge, just as he jumped at the opportunity to take Gus's.

The passing thought left a twinge of pain in its wake, with Minka yearning for his presence on the force. If he'd still been around, she would've known exactly where to turn. They'd taken on the corruption in Atlanta, and in spite of her rookie mistakes, he'd trusted in her and somehow saw her worth.

Her mind drifted back to her mission to rescue Claire…

On the heels of Claire's declaration about Detwiler, Minka called Gus to inform him that she'd located his cousin. She didn't detail Claire's allegations about Detwiler feeding information to a drug ring, but she enlisted his guidance on what to do with the bombshell.

"I can't call the station and report this under his nose, but I'm afraid to wait for his shift to conclude," she told Gus.

"Why don't you get her to safety and let your partner stay behind to secure the area until you return?"

She swallowed hard. "Nobody accompanied me here."

He didn't reprove her disobedience. "Fine. I doubt anybody will disturb the evidence in the time it takes you to get Claire to the hospital. On your way, call the county sheriff so he can get ahead of Detwiler."

"Will do, sir."

"And Officer Parker?"

She braced for discipline. "Yes, sir."

"On behalf of my family, thank you. On behalf of a fellow officer, job well done."

No matter how many years passed, Gus's leadership always boosted her confidence. And because of that first case, she always strived to live up to his expectations.

Absorbed in her nostalgia, she abruptly stumbled on what she needed to do.

Chapter Eleven

Driving up to Gus and Lola's house, Minka's sentimental mood continued when she noted the "Sold" sign in the front lawn. She remembered with fondness helping them move in almost a decade earlier, not long before she and Wes bought their home. Both newly married, the couples were still in that whimsical period of planning their lives together, eager for each fresh chapter. While physically taxing, the weekend was filled with jokes and laughter, a much more light-hearted experience than this moving process had been for the Channings.

When he opened the door, Gus wore the toll from the last week on his face. New shadows circled his eyes and a wrinkle on his forehead she'd never noticed before had appeared. He gave her a fleeting grin.

"Hey. Did Lola enlist your help with packing? I told her I was on it."

"No, she didn't, but I'm willing to offer my services for a couple of hours. You remember how my childhood of being a nomad gave me some serious compacting skills," she replied, trying to lift his spirits. "How are you holding up?"

"By bracing myself between coffee and painkillers."

"You aren't doing as bad as I anticipated, then. I don't want to take much of your time, but I need to bounce something off of you."

"If it's anything other than work, I'm all ears. Otherwise, I'm an unsuitable candidate."

She crossed her arms, leaning on the door jam. "You can tell me that a million times, but I'll never believe it."

Cornered, Gus listened to her discoveries over the last few days, leading up to spotting Liam's car that morning. She acknowledged the holes in her theory, as she had with Cael, but to her frustration, she received a similar response. "Man, I should've just partnered you with Cael."

Sick of the stigma, she threw her head back. "This is not a petty battle between two women. I really think I'm onto something here. Everett's mom was killed, and her murderer never had to pay. Liam's sister died at the hands of a congressman's drunken son, and he all but walked. They're the ultimate team."

"With no evidence in existence."

"I understand that, which is why I'm here. I want you to help me find some and try to expose their scheme."

"Are you insane? My badge is gone, Minka. If I'm caught meddling into police business, I'll be court-marshalled."

"And I won't be far behind you. The new boss took Renee and me off the bombing case."

"Why can't you leave this alone, then?"

"Probably for the same reasons I couldn't leave Claire's abduction alone," she replied with a coy grin. "That turned out pretty well, didn't it?"

"Get back to me on that." He paused to contemplate her proposition. "Like I've admitted before, Renee Hart hasn't been my favorite person, either, but I just don't picture her being a crooked cop."

"And this doesn't mean she is. If Liam is working with Everett, maybe she has no clue. I must say, though, she was quick to declare anyone who surfaced in the investigation as guilty from the get-go. She basically had it out with Tyler Gill at his garage, and you were there when she wanted to ignore the facts and tell the world he was the bomber. I assumed she merely had some crude techniques, but now, I suspect she wanted the investigation to be over before we figured out the truth."

"That seemed odd to me, too, but I still can't shake my doubts," Gus told her.

"The only part I haven't added up is who told Friedman about my suspicions of Everett having a partner. I assumed Renee did it to incite Friedman against you, but if Liam's the accomplice, I doubt she'd chance dangling it out there."

"I'm the one who told him. During one of our last conversations before he ousted me, I fessed up about it in an attempt to prove the flow of communication at the station. As you can deduce, that didn't work." He sighed. "I want to help, believe me, but I'm not sure if I can take the risk. Things aren't great, but they are starting to take a turn for the better. I might have a new job, and we found an apartment nearby it. Plus, the baby…I don't want to make this any harder on us than it's already been."

Minka couldn't fault him for his hesitation. "Where's the new job?"

"Daytona. There's an opening at the hotel Lola's brother manages."

"You're going to work at a hotel? Don't tell me you're going to be a bell boy!" She burst into laughter at the mental image.

"No, Minka. He needs another bouncer at the bar."

"The job you had while you were in the academy? Gus, you're way too overqualified for that."

"I'm not going to be hired at another precinct. My face and dismissal have been all over the news. I couldn't even get a job in mall security."

"Don't waste much time crying over the lack of that prospect, my friend." She patted his shoulder. Aware he would only give her one final appeal, she did her best to speak from the heart. "Eleven years ago, you unwittingly saved me from an awful situation when you made that call to Claire's phone. Despite knowing I was different and witnessing my screw-ups first-hand, you gave me the chance I needed to prove my value. Let me do the same for you."

His eyes softened, but he maintained his stiff posture. "Friedman won't ask me back."

"I wasn't going to get out from behind the desk or coffee machine, either—or so I thought."

He shook his head, telling her that she'd won him over. "Let's drop some boxes off to the storage unit, and then, go see if Liam's car is still at that house."

"Yes, sir."

****

After hauling the boxes from Gus's SUV into the couple's rented storage locker, the two headed over to the diner. They didn't step out to reexamine the possible camera in the window in the event that it was recording. Instead, they stopped to scan the scene for a moment. Minka accessed the photo Finn Steward published and showed it to Gus. Based on the plants near the men, the two investigators agreed the conspirators stood on the corner by the mansion rather than the opposite side, where Dawson's recorder was mounted. The camera Minka spotted was in the ideal position to take such a shot.

After that, they parked behind the diner, one space over from where Wes had done earlier, and spotted the crossover right where it'd been. While it confirmed that what she saw wasn't a fluke, the automobile's presence alone lent nothing more, shaming Minka for a moment.

"Well, there it is," Gus stated.

"Yep." She sank a little into her seat. In attempts to lighten the mood and stall, she dug into her purse and plucked out his least favorite snack. "Want a potato chip?"

He shot her a furrowed brow that told her he caught onto her devious motive.

She snorted. "Oh, that's right. You have an irrational fear of them."

He shook his head as she started to crunch on her snack to irritate him and put his hands on the steering wheel. "Time to go."

"Wait a minute. Whoever's in there has to emerge sooner or later."

"Sure, but it could take six minutes or six days. Lola's going to start worrying if it takes us two hours to unload five boxes. Where does Wes think you are, anyhow?"

"I told him Renee had a pressing lead on a case, which is basically true. I just didn't add that she *is* my lead."

Gus snickered. "You two deserve each other."

Before Minka could conjure up a witty comeback, a black car drove into the vacant lot, its driver familiar. "Renee!" she hissed while the two of them hunched down in perfect synchronization. "What if she recognizes your car?"

"Then, you can call Lola and explain why we're in jail."

Her nerves tensed, but a silver lining occurred to her. "If Renee is working with a wanted terrorist, she can't rat us out. We have messier dirt on her."

"According to whom? Right now, I wouldn't take my chances with Friedman."

Truth be told, neither would she, but she couldn't admit it. Observing Renee step out of her car only fifteen feet in front of them, they slid down even lower but not enough to sacrifice their view. Thankfully, she didn't glance their way, getting into her trunk for a couple of bags of groceries. She carried them around the corner to a back entry, out of their line of sight.

"What do we do?" Minka asked. "Should we move?"

"I don't know; you're the cop here."

"Oh, please! Put on your big boy pants," she replied, invoking a shocked expression to cross his face. "What? I can say that now that you're not my boss. If you don't want me to, think like the lieutenant you are."

He paused, before directing her to get out of the car. They meandered to their right and peeked through the chain link fence between the properties. With Renee already inside, they couldn't discern where she entered, much less who she was visiting. Nonetheless, they waited until she exited just a few minutes later, seeming completely unaware she was under surveillance.

Her hand on her gun, Minka tried to muster the gumption to grab it and announce their presence, but she couldn't. "We missed our moment."

"This time, I'd say it's for the best."

"Should we follow her?"

"Why? If she connected with Everett, that was the incriminating part. Unless her next stop is planting another bomb, there's no point," he said. "Look, my advice to you at this point is to tell Cael and Declan what you observed. As long as it stays between you three, you can even count me as your witness. This should convince them there's something fishy going on, whether it involves Everett or not."

Despite understanding it was the sensible course of action, she had a difficult time accepting it. "This is just so personal."

"Come on, Minka."

"Gus, she's my partner, and she's been playing me this entire time. Our kids were threatened because of her. You lost your career at her hands. Tell me you don't want to follow through on this."

"Of course, I do, but this isn't a game. It's our lives."

"Give me one day," she begged. "If we don't nail this tomorrow, I'll hand it over to Cael."

Trapped yet again, he sighed. "I'm starting to think you should've taken that captains' exam."

****

The next day at work, Minka sat at her desk and debated what to do until the time arrived to execute her plan with Gus. He may not have been her commanding officer at present, but he still gave her an assignment just in case things took a wrong turn. He wanted her to dig up some solid evidence of Renee's involvement, aside from their witnessing her at the mansion. She agreed with his goal, but she had to do some quick strategizing if she wanted to keep to their timetable.

They spent the morning following up on some loose ends pertaining to Friday's grand theft, but to her relief, they stayed close to the precinct. As she researched a lead, the app on her computer synched with her phone kept notifying her of messages. Since she expected to hear from Gus, they all beckoned for her attention. When none proved to be from him, her irritation over the distraction simmered.

Before long, her irritation evolved into inspiration. Aware Renee used the app, too, she devised a way to maximize its benefits.

She feigned a groan—which didn't take major acting skills. "My computer keeps freezing. Could I borrow yours for a minute?"

"Sure. I have to make some calls, anyhow. Mind if I use your extension?" Renee replied.

Minka gave her the go-ahead, figuring the arrangement would only be fair since she'd be secretly on Renee's phone. She switched off her computer monitor so her partner wouldn't notice it ran fine.

They swapped sides of their shared desk, and despite all of the times Minka wanted distance from the woman, Renee's choice not to venture far relieved her. If she strayed off, the app wouldn't stay connected to the phone. With a couple other officers nearby, she opted to open the web browser first, intending to go back to it if anyone approached her.

At last, she clicked on the phone icon, hoping Renee didn't delete her messages as diligently as she did. The long list of text chains showed promise, with Liam's name close to the top. When Minka selected it, the screen displayed the most recent exchanges between the mother and son first. She didn't have to scroll very far before their conversations seemed to concern Everett. Since they wisely never named him, she couldn't make a firm accusation. An hour before Minka and Gus spotted her at the mansion, Liam sent her a grocery list for the unidentified person, but they could claim he was having her shop for his kids when they visited.

Unsatisfied, she skimmed through the chain for something conclusive. She paid keen attention to the day of the bomb threat at Caela's school, but with no activity that morning, she assumed Renee must've called him...unless she disguised her voice and made the threat on her own. Minka didn't allow her mind to dwell on the notion, maintaining a sharp focus. She sifted through more grocery requests, catching onto the fact that Everett was taking full advantage of the situation.

They never discussed the bombing or photo Everett gave Steward, but the messages indicated they didn't have him under their thumbs until after he put it out. Liam mentioned him "throwing a hissy fit" after the bombing and expressed his fear of him going rogue. Minka assumed they caused the tension by holding up his supposed escape plan. At the end of that first week, Liam let on that he scouted out his truck at the souvenir shop and was evidently aware of his history with parking violations. Probably because of his desperation, he broke a bit from his vagueness.

—*He's still hanging out at Cheap R Us. His truck*

is in his favorite illegal spot, so maybe you could give somebody a heads-up. We'd be able to keep better tabs on him if we robbed him of some freedom.—

—I'm on it.—

With that, Minka pulled up Renee's call history and scrolled to the same date. Sure enough, Renee had a conversation that lasted a mere four minutes with the officer who cited Everett. The discovery pleased Minka, but it still didn't give her something to present to Cael without a lot of explanation and suppositions. She peeked at Renee and perceived her patience waning, as she'd completed her business on the phone. Frantic, she returned to the text chain with Liam and speed-read some more messages, until she plucked out the proverbial smoking gun.

—Plan A didn't work out, but I found a better option. He used to be a security guard and knows the place inside and out. He's on board with our cause, too.—

Renee replied with an emoji of the thumbs up sign.

Minka suppressed a cry of glee over the eureka moment. At the same time, she considered how to get it to Cael. Before she arrived at a decision, Renee rose from her seat, jolting Minka out of that quandary and into a new one.

"I'll take my coffee break while you finish up," she said.

As much as she needed the privacy, she needed Renee's phone in close proximity even more. She almost asked to borrow it and claim hers was acting up, but she couldn't use the same line she had about the computer minutes earlier. She couldn't form an alternative quick enough, so she just let her go.

Renee only took a few steps when she received a text. From her husband, it didn't interest Minka at all, but Renee slowed her pace because of the distraction. Minka capitalized on the delay and her preoccupation, seizing her own phone and snapping a picture of the incriminatory messages. She stood and circled the desk.

While Renee lingered nearby, she told her, "Thanks for your help. By the way, I have to go to a parent-teacher conference over my lunch, so I may be a little late getting back."

"No problem. Hope it goes well."

So do I. Minka gazed at the photo she took, then texted Gus to give him the greenlight.

****

Minka hustled out of the station at noon and met Gus at the diner. When she arrived, he'd already placed the order she instructed, so as to not waste time. Though they had much at stake, they agreed to enjoy somewhat of a leisurely lunch. They joked that it could be their last meal in the outside world.

They made idle chit-chat, for the most part, but with their table overlooking the embattled courthouse, the weight of their mission permeated the air. The recurring visits from their flirtatious waitress, however, shifted the meal into another direction for a moment.

"Another cup of coffee, honey?" the curvy woman offered.

"His wife will make him one at home," Minka said.

The lady sauntered away, and Gus rubbed his temple, his face red. "Nice one, Minks. A real ego booster."

"Excuse me, but isn't it Lola's responsibility alone to take care of your ego in that regard?"

His shoulders slumped. "She's hardly looked at me since Friedman cut me loose. My dad's extremely disappointed in me. He read me the riot act when I confessed that I'd failed the exam. Mind you, this is the man who failed second grade. I mean, how do you even do that?"

While unable to stifle a laugh at his comment, she slid her hand across the table to extend a comforting pat on his arm. "I'm really sorry, Gus. He's just used to you surpassing his expectations the way you usually do, and it frazzles him when you don't."

"I guess."

Debating whether or not it would benefit his demeanor, she gave in to her compulsion to share her own anxieties. "Since we're on the subject, my self-esteem has certainly seen better days. The day after you left, Friedman enlightened me on how much he opposed having me on the force. He said that if it weren't for you, I would've never been hired."

Anger flashed in his eyes, before he lowered his head. "He's a dimwitted bigot. I can say that now that he is no longer my boss."

She chuckled at his echoing her sentiment from the day before but returned to her serious tone. "I've always credited my success here to you, but that awful, gut-wrenching conversation I had with him showed me you contributed to it even more than I realized."

He winked. "Maybe initially, but you've made it this far on your own merit."

"Just the same, I'm sometimes tempted to pinch myself because of the fact that you, first of all, gave me a chance in Atlanta. Then, you invited me here in spite of my failure to heed your order to bring backup."

"Even that early in my career, I understood my officers were bound to go rogue once in a while, because I did, too. I counted it as a plus that you fessed up about it."

She gave him a mischievous grin. "I didn't make that mistake twice."

He wagged a finger at her, before he stood and commenced the business ahead of them. "Ready to prove Friedman wrong about both of us?"

Nodding with conviction, she paid the bill and exited the diner. She then stopped right outside the door to call Renee, as Gus listened in with eagerness.

"Detective Hart," Renee greeted.

Minka could only roll her eyes, certain her caller ID would've told her it was her. "Hey, it's me. I'm headed out of the school now, but my friend, Dawson, just alerted me that he noticed Everett in that vacant mansion next to the diner. I guess he's driving a gray crossover. I already texted a few officers to keep their eyes peeled, but I couldn't get ahold of Cael and Declan. Would you mind tracking them down?"

Her shock clear even from afar, Renee fell silent but soon recovered. "I think they're out on another lead."

"I'll keep trying, then," Minka replied, feigning disgust.

"No, don't worry about it. I'll handle it."

She thanked her and hung up. "She took the bait. And you call yourself the expert fisherman."

"The real Minks returns," he teased.

Hurrying around the restaurant to the parking lot, they retreated behind the fence, their attention on Liam's vehicle. It stayed in its usual spot, so while they waited to see what transpired, Minka sent Cael the photo of Renee's texts. A slew of questioning replies bombarded her phone, but she didn't respond, captivated by the sight of Renee barreling into the driveway. A man emerged with a backpack, racing over to meet her. In spite of his dyed black hair, Minka recognized him as Silas Everett.

Everything having led up to this very moment, Minka popped out of her hiding position, and armed, she approached her partner. "Freeze! Both of you."

Still in her car, Renee's head abruptly spun, a caught expression on her face. "Minka?"

"Get out of the car, and drop your gun," she commanded as she jumped over the fence. The detective obeyed, and Minka signaled for her to kick it toward her. "I see that you decided to handle him yourself."

"I know this looks bad, but…"

"But you had a good reason for helping a terrorist flee law enforcement? Does it have anything to do with him driving your son's car?"

Renee lowered her gaze. Silent, she glanced off to the side, before she faced Minka. When she first spoke, her tone was laced with regret, but she gained confidence as she proceeded. "This was Liam's doing—in the beginning, at least. I tried talking him out of it time and again, but he wanted justice for his sister. And you know what? Deep down, so did I. I've given decades of my life seeking it for others, but when it was my turn, the system failed me. All of that time I sacrificed with my children was worth nothing to that judge. He only cared about staying chummy with a politician. Just when I was starting to look forward to

223

my retirement and enjoying my family, that rich, little punk shattered it."

While Minka sympathized with the injustice in her plight, she couldn't reconcile how the woman deemed this a viable solution. "So resorting to terrorism gave you a brighter future? You can kiss your retirement goodbye."

"I never planned this, just like I never planned on losing my only daughter. But accidents happen—just ask Scarlett's killer."

"Was threatening my only child an accident, too?"

Renee offered a timid nod. "In a way. I couldn't let you talk to Tsukino, for fear he'd identify Liam. Caela was never in any danger, though. I didn't want anyone to be hurt in this. That's why I convinced them to plot the bombing at night."

"How kind of you. Who could've guessed a harmless explosion would've resulted in such chaos— where people were hurt?" Directing her attention to Everett, Minka asked him, "Where did you enter into the picture, then?"

"Liam and I met a few months ago at grief counseling and hit it off. When I mentioned being fired from the courthouse, he told me his plan, and I wanted in on it. The legal system betrayed my mama, too."

Minka didn't waste time to gloat over figuring that out. "Why would you give up that photo of you two? Or lure Steward to Froggy Wetlands, only to set off another bomb?"

He gave Renee a sidelong glance. "Just to remind my dear friends of our deal."

"How was bombing the courthouse the solution to all of the injustice you guys have suffered, especially when none of the ones responsible were even there?" Minka questioned.

"It was a message, Minka," Renee said.

"And what message were you sending me this whole time by double-crossing me and trying to coerce me to follow phony leads?"

Renee shrugged. "Don't take it personal. I mean, sure, we took advantage of your lack of finesse from your extended absence, but that's neither here nor there."

Minka restrained her rage from overflowing. "Oh, I doubt that a court of law will judge it that way."

Like they'd planned, Gus appeared and jumped the fence, as well. He waved, his phone in his hand, showing he recorded the entire scene.

Minka advanced to cuff the corrupt detective, until gunfire rang out from the house. She pivoted and observed Gus wincing in pain from the shot that hit his shoulder. He released a shout of agony.

Renee sneered at her former boss. "Sorry, Lieutenant. It must be that unruly son of mine."

Now with three criminals and a wounded friend on her hands, Minka had to make a split decision. Suddenly appearing in the doorway, Liam made the choice for her. He resorted to what started the whole ordeal—an explosion. He threw a stun grenade in their direction, which erupted into a sharp flash of light and deafening roar, sending piercing pains through Minka's ears. After taking out her cochlear transmitter, she struggled to regain her bearings. She recovered just in time to behold the three running to Liam's car.

Before they could drive away, she realized she wasn't on her own. Through her blurry vision, she identified Dawson darting over and tackling Everett to the ground. Meanwhile, she shot a bullet into the car's front and back tires, which forced the other two to retreat into the house. Minka raced after the mother and son, as she instructed Dawson to call 911 for backup. She tossed her handcuffs and Renee's gun to him while he detained Everett.

Following Renee and Liam through the back door, she cautiously treaded up to the main floor. She slowed her pace in an effort to keep the mahogany wood floors from creaking and inched in and out of each room, but she found no one. She started up the majestic, winding staircase, before she noticed a rumble of movement beneath her, indicating that they were in the basement. She scoped out her surroundings for the door that led to it and discovered it to be in the small kitchen.

Holding her breath, Minka opened it and eyeballed Liam on the other side, halfway down the narrow stairway. He spun around and aimed his gun at her. She made the first shot, which landed in his leg. As he dropped down the stairs, the door behind Minka slammed into her. She stumbled down several stairs before she caught her balance, but her weapon slipped out of her hand. Her partner retrieved it, wearing a satisfied grin.

She stood over her, and Minka read her lips as she taunted, "See what I mean by lack of finesse?"

"Killing me will only make your life worse."

"I'm not going to kill you. Your mother doesn't deserve that. Then again, I don't deserve to lose another child, either." Renee put her finger on the trigger. "Help me get my son out of here, for your mother's sake."

The threat barely escaped her lips when Gus

appeared behind her, elbowing her in the side with his uninjured arm and knocking the pistol out of her clutches. He scooped it up as she lunged for it, while Minka scrambled up the stairs to force her to the ground.

"Not bad for a couple of ex-cops and a deaf girl who lacks finesse, huh?" Minka joked, exhausted, as sirens blared into the driveway.

Epilogue

Three Months Later

Donning her dress uniform, Minka brimmed with pride at Gus. Her friend stood on the stage as he was sworn in as a captain. Cael sat at her side with Autumn and fidgety Tyson behind him. Wes and Caela watched the ceremony from behind them as well. Lola, who had three months to go until welcoming her baby girl into the world, accompanied Ryan in the front row; both of them beamed with joy. The road to that perfect moment had been a long one, but on that beautiful April day, Minka considered it all worthwhile.

To top it off, Minka had to grin in observing Chief Friedman. He stood at the podium and sang Gus's praises. At certain points—in true Minka fashion—she gave Cael a subtle nudge over the irony of his statements, but inside, she hoped he had a newfound, genuine respect for Gus. After they arrested Renee, Everett, and Liam, the chief expressed a sincere apology to Gus and reinstated him that very afternoon. He manifested similar regret to her, commending her for the courage and fortitude she displayed in exposing Renee's secret. Even in front of the press, he credited them both with cleansing the department of the traitor among them.

Following the lengthy speech, Lola took the stage

and the honor to assist her husband in swapping his old jacket for one with a second gold bar on his shoulder, signifying his new rank. The sight of him evoked the memory of the day he called her eleven years ago, not long after she rescued Claire…

As Minka munched on her breakfast, her phone rang, and Gus's number illuminated, surprising her a bit, since they hadn't spoken in nearly a month. He'd expressed admiration for her efforts in finding Claire after the take-down, but she figured he was glad to be through with her in light of her rookie mistakes. When he greeted her, his voice revealed no such feelings.

"How's everything going there? Has the city awarded you a medal for uncovering Detwiler's misdeeds?"

She snorted. "Hardly."

She stopped short of admitting the brutal truth that not much had changed in the six weeks that passed since her former captain's arrest. Several of her coworkers began to treat her better, two even taking her as an occasional ride-along, but nobody revered her as a hero or even a so-called normal cop. The new captain didn't voice any plans of giving her a permanent partner or assignment. He didn't send her on many coffee runs and never made her proofread another report, but basically, she still played the part of an intern.

In fact, she stared at the job listings on her computer screen at that very moment, debating what her new dream could be. She panned through other departments that were hiring but wondered if any precinct would treat her differently. She always realized "deaf policewoman" didn't exactly roll off the tongue, but she used to believe she could be the one to change that. To succeed at that, however, she needed someone else to believe in her, too, and maybe she wouldn't find that on the force.

Gus paused, seeming to expect her to elaborate, but when she didn't, he made an announcement. "I had some good news come my way recently. I took the lieutenants' exam, and I passed."

"Congratulations, Gus. I'm so happy for you."

"Thanks. The craziest part is I'm already getting my own precinct, which is what I wanted to run by you. You see, an officer was just promoted to detective to take my place, so that leaves me down one. I was hoping you could fill the spot. We need somebody with your drive, instincts, and determination down here. Would you be interested?"

Trying to contain her excitement, she swallowed the lump in her throat and waited a moment before she gave her answer. "I think I might."

Thrusting Minka out of her nostalgia, the crowd of admirers burst into applause. She cheered along, choking up because of the sentimentality of the day. Once the ceremony concluded, Gus stepped off the platform. Everyone rushed to congratulate him, with his family, particularly his very proud father, first in line.

So as not to intrude on the special moment, Minka held back and visited with others. She and Wes meandered over to Dawson, who'd just accepted a position at the precinct as a part-time crime analyst. After they chatted with him and his wife, her new captain approached her, his face failing to conceal his whirlwind of emotions.

"Captain Channing." She offered him a hug. "That

sounds even better than I expected it would."

"It does to me, too," he agreed. "And I owe it to you."

"I only helped you study a few times."

"You know what I mean. If you hadn't pulled me out of my bullheaded despondency act, I would've been a forty-two-year-old bouncer, living above my in-laws' garage with my pregnant wife and child."

"And if it'd gone wrong, you would've been in prison with me! Pick your poison."

He snickered and nodded. "The point is, you didn't give up on me, and I can't thank you enough for that."

"You don't have to, because you already have. You were the one who taught me all about believing in someone because you believed in me."

He paused, seeming to need a moment to keep a grip on his composure. "But if I may, I'd like to show my gratitude by finally assigning you another partner. Given that your last one was a bit—"

"Corrupt," she bluntly finished for him.

"Yes. Like I was saying, I felt the pressure to find one who suited you well. So, after a thorough search, here's who I've chosen."

Upon his signal, Cael trotted up from behind her, taking his new partner's side.

"You call this thorough?" Minka teased.

"What about Declan?" Wes asked.

"He's decided to partner up with one of the rookies promoted today, and break him in," Gus said. "I'll get to that assignment later, but I wanted this to be my first one as captain."

Joining the clan, Gus's cousin, Claire, strolled over with her husband and son, having flown in for the special occasion. Still a reporter in spite of her traumatic experience in Atlanta, she now wrote for the biggest newspaper in Boston. They all caught up for a short time, before she took out her camera and asked for a photo of the group to put in a piece she was writing.

"It depends on what kind of scathing scheme you're exposing," Gus joked.

She smiled. "Friendship. True friendship."

A word about the author...

Karina Bartow grew up and still lives in Northern Ohio. Though born with cerebral palsy, she's never allowed her disability to define her. Rather, she's used her experiences to breathe life into characters who have physical limitations, but like her, are determined not to let them stand in the way of the life they want. Her works include *Husband in Hiding, Forgetting My Way Back to You, Brother of Interest,* and *Wrong Line, Right Connection.* She may only be able to type with one hand, but she writes with her whole heart! http://www.karinabartow.com